Discovering Her Inheritance

OTHER CROSSRIVER BOOKS
BY DEBRA L. BUTTERFIELD

FICTION

Claiming Her Inheritance, book 1 of Her Inheritance series
Discovering Her Inheritance, book 2 of Her Inheritance series
Embracing Her Inheritance, book 3 of Her Inheritance series
Mystery on Maple Hill, a short story

NONFICTION

Self-editing & Publishing Tips for Indie Authors
7 Cheat Sheets to Cut Editing Costs
Unshakable Faith, a Bible study
Unshakable Faith Leaders Guide
Carried by Grace: a guide for mothers of victims of sexual abuse

COMPILED AND EDITED

Abba's Promise: 33 Stories of God's Pledge to Provide
Abba's Answers: 30 Stories of God's Answers to Prayer

Discovering Her Inheritance

Debra L. Butterfield

St. Joseph, MO USA

DISCOVERING HER INHERITANCE
Copyright © 2023 Debra L. Butterfield

ISBN: 978-1-936501-85-4

Scripture quotations are taken from the Holy Bible, New Living Translation, copyright ©1996, 2004, 2007, 2013 by Tyndale House Foundation. Used by permission of Tyndale House Publishers, Inc., Carol Stream, Illinois 60188. All rights reserved.

Scripture taken from the New King James Version®. Copyright © 1982 by Thomas Nelson. Used by permission. All rights reserved.

For more information on Debra L. Butterfield, visit DebraLButterfield.com

Cover art: iStock.com/Riekkinen
Cover design: Debra L. Butterfield

Printed in the United States of America.

"LORD, you alone are my inheritance, my cup of blessing."
Psalm 16:5a NLT

Chapter One

"You will show me the way of life." Psalm 16:11a NLT

The report of gunfire sent me diving off my horse. As I hit the ground, I rolled and began searching for a place to take cover. A small boulder next to a scrubby bush looked promising. I scurried over and scrunched my body as best I could behind the rock, then scanned the surrounding area for the shooter. Nothing in front of me or to my left or right flank. Where were my fellow Marines? I turned over on my back and checked out my six. Nothing behind me.

That's when I noticed it.

Blood soaked my desert camo jacket. I've been shot? But I don't feel a thing.

I ripped open my uniform and found the bullet hole in my now-red undershirt. I should be dead. How could I be anything but, having taken a bullet direct to my heart. Maybe I was. Yet blood continued to rapidly pulse from that gaping hole. That wouldn't be happening if I was dead. This scenario certainly didn't fit my idea of heaven or hell. I couldn't be dead.

I watched, paralyzed, as blood saturated my undershirt.

Yet I didn't feel anything.

I didn't feel a thing.

Not a thing.

I bolted up in bed, my pajamas drenched with sweat. Using the sheet, I wiped my face dry and took several slow breaths. I threw the

7

covers off, rose and peeled my wet pj's loose, then went to the kitchen for a glass of water.

Nothing about that dream made sense. I retreated to my favorite chair in the living room. My damp pajamas brought on a chill, so I pulled down the fleece blanket I kept draped over the back of the chair and wrapped myself in it. Then I grabbed my journal from beside the chair and started analyzing the components of my dream.

I was on a horse in the open prairie of Montana.

Inheriting 33 percent of a multi-million-dollar cattle ranch from Chase Reynolds Jr. back in August had baptized me into a world of luxury. Ten days on horseback, driving cattle across the open prairies of Montana had hypnotized me with the state's beauty and serenity. So being on a horse in Montana made sense.

But I was in uniform. And getting shot at made sense in that context because, after all, Marines in the middle of a war get shot at. But I should have been in a Humvee in the blistering desert of the Middle East, not riding a horse. Besides, I'd left the Corps over twenty years ago.

While I was at the Reynold's ranch, the foreman had attempted to kill me three times, one of which included a shot from a rifle. Everything about the dream spoke Montana.

Why was my head mixing up past and present events? If I'd had this dream back in August when the first attempt on my life at the ranch occurred, that'd be different. But now, nearly two months later? What was happening in my life right now that precipitated this dream?

Heavenly Father, are You trying to tell me something? If so, help me understand what it is.

For several minutes, I sat and listened for the Lord's voice within my spirit but heard nothing. Maybe I was asking the wrong question.

I turned my attention to the last element of the dream. Not feeling any pain from the bullet that had penetrated my heart plagued me more than anything else about the dream. Wounded and bleeding out. I should have been dead but wasn't. If I hadn't seen the pool of blood, I'd never have known I'd been shot.

"Sally. Sally. Wake up."

"Hmm? What?" I opened my eyes to find Abby, my twin sister, hovering over me. Gray streaked her wavy brown hair at her left temple, the same place as mine. I suppose hers was more pronounced because it cascaded past her shoulders and mine was barely an inch long.

"What are you doing in the living room?"

"I had a nightmare and came out here to think." I shrugged and sat up. "Guess I fell back to sleep. What time is it?"

"Quarter to nine—"

"Quarter to nine! I'd better get my rear in gear if we're going to be at Pendrake's by ten."

"If I'd realized you weren't in bed to hear your alarm, I'd have wakened you sooner."

"It's not your fault. Maybe today's meeting is what prompted my nightmare." I stood, folded the blanket, and tossed it over the back of the chair. "The drive to Pendrake will take thirty to thirty-five minutes. I'll get showered and dressed. Can you fix me a coffee to go?"

"Sure."

I rushed off to my bedroom. Was my proposal to buy Pendrake going to get shot down?

"This is nerve-racking," I told Abby. After more than a month of research, planning, and writing a buyout offer, Abby, my potential business partners Jennifer Maxwell and her husband, John, and I now stood in the lobby of Pendrake Publishing, awaiting the meeting that would pronounce their decision on our offer.

"Relax and take a seat" Abby said. "They'll say yes or they'll say no."

I stopped my pacing. I looked at Jen and John seated comfortably in the reception area leather chairs, John busily texting. Abby sat on a leather sofa sipping coffee. I took a seat next to her. "Good point, Abby.

I'm frustrated with this wait. We were told ten o' clock, and it's now ten-thirty. Is this their idea of a power play?"

"Maybe on Berkeley's part," Jen said. "Don't give him the satisfaction of seeing you bothered."

Jen and I had worked together at Pendrake's for fifteen years. We'd become like sisters despite her being eight years younger. I could always count on her to encourage me.

I looked around the lobby for Berkeley Snyder, the current CEO of Pendrake. It was Berkeley's micro-management and penchant for publishing erotica that had driven me to quit Pendrake.

"You're right, Jen." I cleared my throat and continued. "Before we go into that boardroom, I want you each to know how much I appreciate you and the work you put into this idea."

"It's been our pleasure," John said. "We want to see this happen too."

The perky receptionist approached us. A new hire, obviously; she hadn't been working at Pendrake three months ago when I quit my job. She looked sixteen. "The board is ready to see you now." Her high heels clicked rhythmically across the tile floor as she led us to the boardroom and opened the door for us to enter.

I had dressed in my best black business suit with a red shirt and white scarf in an attempt to display my self-assurance. In truth, it had deserted me several months ago when Pendrake's founder and my mentor died and Berkeley Snyder came aboard. To give me the confidence and boldness I needed as I entered the room, I imagined myself in my Marine Corps dress blues decked out with my military ribbons and awards.

The board members, all men, sat on one side of the conference table. It appeared they had already been conducting business. They reminded me of Marine Corps officers planning a battle strategy. Formidable.

Jen, John, Abby, and I took the empty seats across from them.

Jen, in a cream suit with a black shirt, sat to my right. Abby looked stunning, as always, in a soft pink pantsuit and sat to my left. John, the lawyer of our little group, was like the cherry on top. He looked dashing as ever in an iron gray suit, arctic white shirt, and beige tie.

He exuded aplomb—I hoped I did too. I had no doubt he kept the rapt attention of jurors during any trial.

Add the seven board members all dressed in black or gray suits, white shirts, and ties and you'd have thought the power brokers of New York had come to take over Kansas City. The chairman rapped his gavel and called everyone to order. After the board members stopped their chatter, the chairman turned to face me.

"Miss Clark, thank you for your offer to buy Pendrake. It's a decent one, but quite frankly, we like the increased profits Mr. Snyder has brought to the company. We believe those profits will increase considerably in the coming year. So, we're declining your offer."

I glanced over at Jen and John. They kept poker faces. I tapped into my Marine Corps MP training in an effort to do the same. I'm not sure what I expected to occur at this meeting, but I most certainly didn't expect it to be over and done in less than five minutes.

I straightened my back and leaned forward. "Mr. Snyder's increased profits have come through publishing erotica. Is that the kind of reputation you want for Pendrake, Mr. Cockrell?"

"Profits are profits, Miss Clark. I can, however, extend the offer Mr. Snyder made to you back in August. To be the director of a new imprint that will focus on spiritual books."

Spiritual. Today's buzzword that meant everything religious except for Christianity. I sensed a check in my spirit and glanced at Abby. The frown on her face communicated she had the same check.

"Sir, my faith and my conscience won't allow me to accept your offer." I plastered on a smile and stood. "Thank you for your time and the board's consideration." I reached across the table to shake his hand. I nodded to the other board members around the table, and then Jen, John, Abby, and I filed out of the room.

"That door's closed, in more ways than one," I said as the boardroom door clicked closed with finality behind me. "But I'm glad it's over. I know it's a little early, but can I take you all to lunch? We can discuss our next option."

"I've got to get back to work. I have court to prepare for," John said.

He leaned over and gave Jen a kiss on the cheek. "I'll grab a sandwich on my way to the office. See you later, hon."

We watched as John walked through the lobby and out the door.

"How about it, you two, you up for lunch?" I asked. "Besides being too nervous to eat breakfast, I overslept and didn't have time. I'm hungry."

"If I remember correctly, this new business journey started out over a discussion during lunch at Wendy's." Jen grinned and linked arms with Abby and me. "Let's make it a tradition."

To those around us, we probably appeared to be traveling down the yellow brick road as we giggled our way out the building and headed to lunch.

"I've got so many questions buzzing around my head." I started the car and pulled out of the parking lot and into the typical wild rush of Kansas City's traffic. "I'm disappointed the board turned down our offer, yet mostly I'm relieved. I admit I didn't have total peace about it. That alone should have told me not to pursue it. Plus, I don't want to stay here in Kansas City, and that alleviates the task of moving the business somewhere else."

"And now the door to start our own company is wide open," Jen pronounced from the back seat.

"Yes! We probably should have gone in that direction all along. God's got something great planned. I'm sure. He hasn't yet told me what it is." I maneuvered the car through traffic and thought back to my nightmare. Was it prophetic about my buyout of Pendrake or did it have a deeper meaning? Maybe I wasn't destined to go into business for myself at all.

"Abby, how hard is it to build from the ground up?" Jen asked.

"Starting any business can be challenging, and there are so many scenarios that could affect your success." Abby paused and through the corner of my eye, I could see her tapping her lips as she thought. "I'm sure publishing books has its similarities to publishing a magazine, but I know nothing about book distribution. At the magazine, we know exactly who we're trying to reach—ranchers—and where to find them. Can you say that about selling books?"

"I know acquisitions and editing," Jen said, "but I'd have to pick the brains of our sales and marketing teams to learn about sales and distribution."

We arrived at Wendy's and I parked the car. It was barely eleven, so the usual lunch rush hadn't quite begun. We placed our order and got our drinks. "It's Friday, and a slew of people will fill this place in the next half hour. Let's find a remote corner table."

By then our orders were ready. We grabbed our trays and made our way to a table. We settled ourselves and I said a prayer.

"Sally, I know you're not going to like this." Jen frowned, then sighed as she sat down. "John's having second thoughts about leaving Kansas City. He's looking at a possible partnership with the law firm."

"Really? That's great, Jen! Good for him. When will he find out?"

"That's the tough part. Not until January. I'm surprised Pendrake's board decided as quickly as they did. Thanksgiving is only six weeks away. I figured they'd put the decision off until after the holidays."

"On a side note. Are you going to quit Pendrake?" I bit into my spicy chicken sandwich.

"Yes," Jen said adamantly. "I haven't put in my two-week notice yet, but I'll do that this afternoon as soon as I get back from this lunch. Like you, my faith and conscience have been prodding me."

"What are you going to do instead?" Abby asked.

"I think I might start freelance editing."

"Does John's possible partnership affect the one you'd have with Sally? I detect a bit of hesitation on your part."

"Not at all, Abby. I'm just not certain how well it would work with Sally in one place and me in another."

"Yeah, I've had some hesitation about that myself." I took a gulp of water to cool my burning tongue. "And at this point, I don't know where I want to move to. I want to find something that offers more country living like what I grew up with and a ton less traffic."

"The ranch at Great Falls certainly offers that." Abby wiggled her eyebrows at me and then bit into a french fry.

"Yes, it does. But I love Missouri's long summers." I stirred the ice in my drink. With every stir, my spirit swirled around as if caught in a tornado. My whole life had felt that way since back in late July when I first learned of my inheritance and that Abby was my sister.

"And the man that comes with Montana?" Jen teased. "Is he not enough of an enticement?"

"The man?" Abby tipped her head to the right and looked up, then it dawned. "Oh! You mean my brother, Chase."

I shivered and my gut tensed at the mention of Chase. "That suggestion is scarier than Montana winters. Yes, I like Chase and he likes me—I'm so glad he's only your brother by adoption, Abby—but I'm torn about a romance developing between us."

Too many Marines had come on to me. They wanted sex on the first date. No thank you. I had risked my heart once and it got trampled on. I stared down at my half-eaten spicy chicken. Bad memories seared my heart the way that sandwich did my mouth. I shook the memories from my head and plopped a french fry into my honey mustard sauce.

"I'm more concerned about God's direction for my life than what kind of relationship might develop between me and Chase. God threw me a real curve ball with this inheritance. It's an amazing blessing, and I'm excited, but also floundering…a lot. I feel such a weight of responsibility. God brought this for a reason, and I want to be a good steward of this money."

The conversation lulled for several minutes as we ate. I imagine Abby and Jen were contemplating how they might answer me.

Jen broke the silence. "I wish I had an answer for you. You could live a life of leisure if you wanted."

"I *am* pushing sixty. I could retire, but I think I'd get bored with that. I might be fifty-eight, but I'm too young to sit around doing nothing all day. We all are." We laughed and wholeheartedly agreed we were all still twenty-somethings.

"Have you considered offering something other than publishing?" Abby said. "Why not a partnership in an editing business. That might work better remotely than publishing. And what about writing? You have money enough now that you could write books full time. Maybe co-author with Jen."

I leaned back in my seat and contemplated Abby's words. She sat grinning at me, her arms crossed.

"That's a terrific idea." Jen's eyes grew wide, shining with excitement, and her eyebrows rose. She put down her grilled chicken, wiped her hands on her napkin, then reached over to cup my hands in hers. "Open yourself up to the possibilities God might have for you. You inherited a lot of money, but maybe the *real* inheritance is the family He brought you. This amazing twin sister! Her brother. All those nieces and nephews. I know you, and you're so afraid of getting hurt, you can't see what a blessing that is."

I sat dumbfounded. I looked at Abby for confirmation, but was unable to read the message in her eyes. I opened my mouth to say something, then shut it again.

"Jen is a great friend to you, Sally. Cherish that. Wisdom resides in what she just said." Abby side hugged me and smiled. "God will show you the way. Don't make any major decisions until you're positive you've heard from Him. Where Chase is concerned, just be yourself. Whether that relationship is as brother and sister or something more, God will lead you."

I thought about Chase Reynolds III, Abby's brother by virtue of her adoption into the Reynolds family when she was a baby. He was only three years older than I was and ran the Double R Ranch of which I'd inherited 33 percent from his father. Back in August, Chase had told me he thought he was falling in love with me. No one had ever said those words to me. They shocked me. We had done nothing but spar with each other and had known each other only four weeks. How could anyone say they were falling in love after such a short time? To give him credit, he wasn't sure himself and he made that clear. Then and now, I struggled to trust the honesty of his proclamation.

"Listen, Sally, why don't you take the holidays and go visit your new family?" Jen withdrew her hands from mine and leaned back. "Spend time in prayer and seek God's direction. You know He has a plan. Have you asked Him what it is?"

"I have asked God about His plan, but I haven't heard any answers yet." A smile broke my lips. "But last night, Abby reiterated Chase's invite to spend the holidays with them in Great Falls. So maybe your suggestion is a confirmation that I should go."

"Well, I say you accept Abby's invite." Jen encouraged me.

"I second that," Abby chimed. "You can rest, relax, spend time with God. You can stay with me in town, but I'm sure Chase would be fine if you stayed at the ranch. You know the solitude will rejuvenate you."

"True."

"And don't forget about Sandy and all the other horses. They miss you."

"That's dirty pool, Abby. You know I love being with the horses."

"That should tell you, you belong in Great Falls," Jen said.

I sighed. Life had been chaotic, to say the least, since I learned about the inheritance and discovered Abby was my twin sister in the bargain. Lately, God had certainly made life an adventure. "Okay, you two, you've convinced me. We'll see what God and Montana have in store for me."

Chapter Two

"Keep me safe, O God, for I have come to
you for refuge." Psalm 16:1 NLT

I can hardly wait for the holidays. It'll be so much fun having you at the ranch," Abby said as we entered my apartment after lunch. "I'll let Chase know you're coming once we firm up the plans."

I plopped down on the couch, already second-guessing my decision. Seven weeks at the Double R would certainly give Chase and me time to determine what direction our relationship might go. When Chase first told me he'd begun to love me, the idea kind of appealed to me, yet unnerved me too. Why consider a romantic relationship if marriage wasn't the end result? And marriage? I hated that idea.

"Why the big frown? Aren't you excited about coming to the ranch?" Abby asked.

"Sure I am. I was thinking about Chase, and a romantic relationship, and marriage. All my father ever did was boss my mom around. I don't need or want a man telling me what to do every day. And that's all marriage is."

"No, Sally, it most definitely isn't. A godly marriage is about trust and love and putting the needs of your spouse ahead of your own. I see that happening between Jen and John, and I've only known them a few short weeks. Haven't you ever noticed it?"

"No, can't say that I have."

"I'd say the Lord has some refining to do in your life in the coming months." Abby sat next to me on the couch.

"Not sure I like the sound of that."

"Listen, in marriage, wives are to submit to their husbands. Still, it's the wife's choice to submit or not, but a marriage won't flourish without it. The foundation is the trust you have in your husband. I would think having been a Marine that you'd understand submission. After all, you agreed to submit to their authority when you enlisted."

"There again, like everything else in life, you do as you're told or suffer the consequences."

"But, Sally, you always have a choice. Submission isn't mutely obeying whatever you're told. God gave Adam a woman as a helpmate, not as a yes man. You speak your opinion, discuss the situation, and come to a mutual decision. Marriage isn't a relationship of owner and slave."

"What little teaching I've heard in church on submission never explained it that way."

"It's possible you didn't have ears to hear."

"What's that mean?"

"It means your heart," Abby tapped my chest, "your spirit, wasn't open to hearing God's truth. Submission is a function of the heart, not your will."

"Hmm. But isn't submitting a choice, and choice a part of my will?"

"You can make a choice to submit, but still be rebellious within your heart. Like when you were a kid. You did what your father told you, but deep down you were fighting against him. Does that make sense?"

"Yeah, it does. Lots of food for thought." This conversation challenged my comfort level for personal confessions; time to change the subject. "Listen, I can't let you leave Missouri without experiencing the Big Muddy. Pumpkin fest begins tonight in St. Joe, and their Riverfront Park offers the best view of the river I know in this area. We can drive up tomorrow, take in the festival, and do some sightseeing."

"The Big Muddy, huh? Sounds like a nasty watering hole with cattle lolling around in it." She laughed. "I'm game, if you are."

I hadn't expected Abby to let our conversation on submission drop so easily. I suspected the topic would surface again in the not-too-distant future.

###

"I'm telling you, Sally, Chase is smitten with you." Abby entered my sun-drenched kitchen, putting a damper on my enjoyment of my coffee flavored with Irish Crème creamer.

I reeled at her comment. "It's six o' clock on a Saturday morning, and you're talking about love?" Even though she was my twin sister, I had only just discovered that fact two months ago. I was still getting to know her and couldn't quite determine how serious she was. "Are you being serious or just joking around?" A love-smitten Chase and an amazing inheritance. What would God bring next?

"I'm serious. I know Chase. Since you left the ranch back in September, he's talked about you nearly every day."

"What's *not* to talk about? A perfect stranger inherits a third of the Reynolds ranch and turns out to be your twin sister. And let's not forget, you learned you were adopted. If it was me, I'd be talking too. But I'm sure you're wrong about him being *smitten* with me." I glanced at the clock on the wall. "It's an hour drive to St. Joe. Let's leave by 8:30 so we can watch the kids in the costume parade."

"If the pumpkin fest means enjoying pumpkin spice lattes and pumpkin pie all day long, then let's get started."

"I'm sure we'll find those somewhere. We'll be doing plenty of walking, so wear comfortable clothes and shoes. You know, that's the second time in less than twenty-four hours that you let drop the subject of Chase. Do you have some devious plan to blindside me later on?"

"Don't be ridiculous. I'll give you plenty of fair warning." She flashed me a mischievous grin.

I laughed. "That's good to know."

###

As we drove north to St. Joseph, I-435's Saturday morning traffic sped to the KCI Airport, vying for top position like Mario Andretti at the Indy 500. As I expected, the cars thinned dramatically once we passed the airport exit. I sighed my relief. The craziness of KC traffic seemed to get worse every year.

"Even though my offer to Pendrake fell through, your advice was priceless. Thanks so much." It wasn't merely Abby's business acumen I was thankful for. The inheritance from her father made the whole deal possible.

"I was more than glad to help. It might have been your idea, but I encouraged it. And I'm very glad you felt comfortable enough to call and ask. With Jake and Leslie's turmoil, getting away from Great Falls for a while appealed to me."

"How are Leslie and Jake?"

"Leslie's having a hard time, I think. She's taken a sabbatical. Jake is still being evaluated for competency to stand trial. My heart aches for Leslie, and she's only my niece. I can't imagine what Chase must be feeling watching his daughter face the turmoil of her husband being tried for attempted murder."

"It's been a month since his arrest. How long does an evaluation last?"

"As long as it takes, I guess. What about you? It isn't every day someone tries to kill you. Did that create any problems?" A frown creased Abby's lips.

"I faced worse while in the Marine Corps, but Jake's attempt on my life did trigger some flashbacks from my time in the Middle East. I talked with my VA counselor about it." I repositioned myself in my seat and checked my mirrors as I prepared to merge onto I-29. An eighteen-wheeler was barreling down the hill. I slowed and shifted into fifth gear, letting him whiz by before merging. "With Leslie out, who's running things at the magazine?"

"Emily is. She does a fine job, much more level-headed than Leslie."

"Do you think I'll have to come back to Great Falls to testify against Jake?"

Abby shifted in her seat. "I have no idea. But I think we'd all like to see you move to Great Falls, not just come for a visit. Chase wants you back, and all my nephews rave about how the horses responded to you. How can I convince you to move to Montana?"

"Can you change the weather?" I snickered. "I'm not crazy about below zero temperatures or winters that last six months." The plethora of Missouri's maple, oak, and sycamore trees boasted their peak fall colors of red, orange, and gold. It would be well after Halloween before any stood bare. Many of the corn and soybean fields had yet to be harvested. Jack Frost hadn't shown his face either. Could Montana say that?

"Winter in Great Falls isn't like that. I'm sure you get below zero temps in Kansas City too." Abby looked out the window at the passing fields. "I have to admit, Great Falls isn't as green or humid as it is here. These trees are gorgeous. Most of ours reach their peak colors in mid-September. But if the weather is your only objection, convincing you to move might not be that hard."

Abby watched the scenery as we continued north. Plenty of cars zipped past me, and I wondered where they were all going. St. Joe struck me as more of a farming community, and I couldn't imagine KC residents flocking there for an entertaining weekend. Omaha, maybe, but not St. Joe.

"I think you're trying to convince me to fall in love with Chase. Have you forgotten how much we fought while I was there? We might end up killing each other before we got past our first date." Abby had let that conversation drop this morning, now here I was bringing it up again. Why? Was I genuinely interested in Chase?

"Don't be ridiculous. You both are stubborn people, that's all."

"Well, no matter how Chase feels about me, I'm not giving up my independence."

"What makes you think being in a relationship means doing that?"

"I thought that was obvious, Abby. I couldn't just up and decide to take a weekend trip somewhere. Even going out to dinner would require consulting someone about where to go."

"That's true enough, but remember what I said about submission yesterday?"

"Yeah, I do. But you've never been married, so how do you know what it's really like?" Memories of my father's violent outbursts rang in my ears. The topic of marriage triggered deep childhood wounds in me, wounds that, if I was honest with myself, had never healed.

"Because I saw it modeled by my own parents. They were a wonderful example of a biblical marriage."

"As bossy as my father was, I often wondered why Mom married him. If you want me to move to Montana, you'll have better luck if you don't include Chase in the equation."

"I'm sorry your father has had such a negative impact on you."

"Not just my father. Men and I have never gotten along. You know my adoptive father was abusive, the boys in high school took no interest in me, and Marines only wanted sex."

Abby shook her head and sighed. "I'm glad I was able to help you open up to God's love for you. He expects men to love their wives like Christ loved the church."

"Why haven't you ever married?"

"I've been quite content being single. So tell me more about this Pumpkin Festival."

"I'm not letting you off that easy. If you're content being single, why do you want to marry me off? Aren't I allowed to be content as a single woman?"

Abby laughed. "Of course. But you seem to be discontent about everything in your life."

"Touche. Only since everything changed at work when Mr. Pendrake died. My discontent is a subject for another time." I hit the blinker and pulled into the left lane to pass a semi. "I haven't been to Pumpkin Fest in several years. It gets me away from the hecticness—is that a word?—of the KC crowds and into nature. St. Joe does it every year the second weekend of October. Takes place at the park across the street from the Pony Express Museum. The Pony Express is one of St. Joe's claims to fame. It started there. I thought the museum might be something you'd enjoy."

"Sure. Tell me more about the festival."

"It's like most are, various events and vendors selling their wares. Different bands play most of the day. The highlight is the lighting of

Pumpkin Mountain, carved pumpkins rigged with little electric lights inside them and set up on several tiers of scaffolding. Once it's dark outside, the crowd gathers and counts down from ten and all the pumpkins are lit at once. Nothing spectacular, but I think it's sorta fun."

"Like lighting a town Christmas tree?"

"Yeah, exactly."

Abby chuckled. "I can't imagine Leslie attending."

"Me either." I belly laughed as I envisioned Abby's only-the-best-for-me sophisticated niece sitting on a hay bale staring at a scaffold of carved pumpkins while gingerly plucking bits of hay from her clothes. I worked to catch my breath. "I needed that laugh. Thanks. We'll visit the Remington Nature Center too. It's by the river, with a walking trail that gives an up-close-and-personal view of the Missouri River. It's so much different than the Missouri headwaters of Montana."

"If St. Joseph is anything like all these lush colorful trees and rolling fields I'm seeing, I'm sure I'll enjoy it. And I don't care what we do as long as we're doing it together. I'm really going to miss you when I go home. I'll be counting the days until you come for Thanksgiving." A hint of sadness tinted Abby's voice.

"Me too. I know you've been here three weeks already, but I wish you could stay another three."

"I'm praying your holiday stay will help convince you Montana winters aren't as bad as you think they are."

"Possibly. Personally, I like looooong hot summers." We drove the remaining twenty minutes to St. Joseph in silence, with me contemplating whether Chase Reynolds and Montana were a part of my future.

Though I'd already spent a considerable amount of time in prayer, I hadn't heard from God about His plans for me. Waiting on His answers had to be the hardest part of living my faith.

He would answer. I was certain of that. But would I like the answer when it arrived?

Chapter Three

"I have set the LORD always before me." Psalm 16:8a KJV

The scent of wet dirt, river water, and plants brought peace to my soul. I inhaled slowly and reveled in the song of nature—the subtle rush of the Missouri River as it flowed south to join the Mississippi, birds chirping, bugs buzzing. My trip to the Reynolds' ranch back in August had reawakened my love of nature. I could hardly wait to get out of the noise and chaos of people that civilization called Kansas City.

Abby and I had just finished touring the Remington Nature Center, and now we stood along the eastern shore of the Big Muddy. I quoted some stats I knew about the river, and Abby was duly impressed with its width, depth, rapid flow, muddy color, and how often it flooded.

"I've glanced down at the river the few times we've crossed the bridge in Kansas City and noted its mucky color. But here in St. Joseph, it seems even darker than in Kansas City," Abby said.

"Back in August during the cattle drive at the ranch, one of the boys mentioned washing in the river since it was the only water available while out on the range. I had to laugh because this is the river I pictured. I couldn't imagine getting clean by bathing in water like this."

"I agree. Let's walk the trail and enjoy this beauty."

"Sure." We walked in silence for several minutes.

"You seem lost in thought," Abby said.

"Yeah. Thinking about what God has for me in the coming months.

Not knowing makes me feel like being on that river with no paddles or rudder to steer with."

"But you can trust God to guide your every step. One step at time, one day at a time. Keep your eyes on Jesus and let the Holy Spirit lead you."

"Abby, you're so right. I needed that reminder. Walk by faith, fully persuaded that what God has promised, He is able to do. I'm so glad He brought us together!" I gave her a long hug, and we continued our hike.

Our Saturday disappeared quickly as we played tourist in St. Joseph. Sunday consisted of church and dinner with Jen and John. Now as Monday began, Abby prepared to head back to Great Falls.

"What time tomorrow does your pilot fly in to pick you up?" I asked. No sooner had the words left my mouth when my cell phone rang.

"He told me to be ready to leave by one," Abby said while I retrieved my phone from the end table next to the couch.

"Hello?" I answered.

"Is this Sally Clark?" a man asked.

"Yes, this is Sally. Who's this?"

"I'm Sergeant Kowalski from the Nebraska Department of Corrections. I'm sorry to inform you your father has died."

My father was dead?

I was glad I was sitting. My father had led a tortured life—some demon had pushed him into embracing alcohol to numb his pain and eventually committing murder. Now more than likely, he'd gone on to more torture.

I looked at Abby.

"What's wrong?" she mouthed.

"My father died," I told her, then turned my attention back to Sgt. Kowalski. Abby hugged my shoulders as I continued the phone call. "Can you tell me how he died?"

"Heart attack, according to the paperwork I have."

"Since he was a prisoner there, does the state bury him or is that my responsibility?"

"He requested burial in Scottsbluff, Nebraska. Our paperwork states he has a plot in Fairview Cemetery."

I listened intently as Sgt. Kowalski explained things. I scribbled notes as quickly as I could.

"Thank you for calling, Sergeant. I'll notify a mortuary in Scottsbluff and get the ball rolling to have my father's body transported. Thank you again for calling." I ended the call and pocketed my phone. So it would seem my adoptive father, who spent years telling me how much he didn't want me, now needed me.

Shock and anger choked me. I closed my eyes, dropped my head back, and took a deep breath.

"Abby, I'm so glad you were here. Your presence kept me level-headed. I was tempted to tell the sergeant I couldn't care less what they did with my father's body," I scoffed. "Obviously I haven't truly forgiven him."

"Sally, I'm so sorry. I know how you feel about him, but you'll still grieve his death." Abby squeezed my shoulder. "No one deserves a prison burial."

"I guess so. I've got to find a funeral home in Scottsbluff and make the necessary arrangements for his body to be picked up from the prison and transported. It's hard to believe he has a burial plot."

"My guess is that's it right next to your mom. Didn't you tell me he started on the alcohol when she died? He must have loved her very much."

"Could you make a pot of coffee? It will help steady my nerves." I snatched the notes I'd made and went to my computer in the office to research Fairview Cemetery. It looked nice. I did a search for other funeral homes to do some price comparisons, then realized that was an unnecessary task. I wouldn't know a good price from a bad one, and I didn't need to worry about money. Besides, if he had a plot, maybe he had already made pre-paid funeral arrangements as well.

While I was jotting down the number for Fairview, Abby joined me in the office. She held out a steaming cup of coffee, my equivalent of a stiff drink. "Thanks." I took the cup from her.

Abby had one for herself as well. She set it on the desk and pulled up a chair next to me. "You know, if he had a plot, it's possible he wrote a will. Did the sergeant mention one?"

"Yes." I grabbed my notes. "He said to contact Kurt Schwartz, but the phone number he had for the guy wasn't any good. Could you do some research on him while I call the funeral home?"

"Of course."

I relinquished my seat at the computer, Abby took my place, and we set to work. When it was all said and done, the funeral for my father was arranged for this coming Thursday at 10 a.m.

"Any luck locating Mr. Schwartz?"

"No. I suggest you do some research when you get to Scottsbluff. Or call the funeral home back and ask if they know him," Abby said.

"I think I'll wait until I get there." I swallowed the last mouthful of coffee and stared into the empty cup for a moment, then looked over at Abby. " I know you're supposed to fly home tomorrow, but would you consider coming to Scottsbluff with me? I could use your calming support. Maybe Steve can fly there and get you after the funeral."

"I have an even better idea." She grinned and her eyes sparkled with mischief. "Why don't we simply drive to Great Falls after the funeral?" She turned to the computer and pulled up Google maps. "Look, Scottsbluff is almost halfway to Great Falls."

I opened my mouth to protest, but Abby held up her hand to stop me.

"No protests allowed."

"How do you know I was going to protest?"

"I could see it on your face." She raised her eyebrows at me.

I laughed. "Thanksgiving is more than a month away. Won't you get tired of having me around for the next two-and-a-half months?"

"Not at all."

I considered the idea, tipping my shoulders up and down as I thought. The suggestion excited me. "Let's do it!"

###

Two days later I rolled out of bed energized about being back in Scottsbluff and the coming weeks in Montana. Being in Nebraska might be a bit nostalgic and fun. I hadn't returned home since leaving for Marine Corps boot camp forty years ago.

I glanced over at my suitcases. The Stetson cowboy hat Chase had given me sat on top of them. Had I packed enough sweaters and thermal underwear to keep me warm? I showered, dressed, and made my way to the kitchen. Abby already had the coffee brewed. As I poured my first cup, she entered the kitchen, her suitcases in tow.

"Good morning," I chirped. "Are you ready to hit the road?"

"I am. I've had fun here with you, but I'm ready to get home to my own bed."

We loaded my Chevy Cruze, then poured ourselves each a cup of coffee to go. The clock on the car dash read 6:00 a.m. when I pulled out of the driveway. Good thing Abby was a morning person like me. The usual KC traffic still slept soundly in bed. Shoot, even the sun had barely opened his eyes.

When we passed the exit for KCI Airport, the road became ours alone. My thoughts drifted, and I half wondered how much my hometown had changed in forty years. I'd lost all connection to my high school friends. Would there be any of Mom's or Father's friends who would remember me or my parents?

"Thanks for coming with me, Abby. I really appreciate it. I know you probably preferred to fly home. It'll be two hard days on the road to get to Great Falls, even with stopping in Scottsbluff."

"I was more than glad to come, so don't give it a second thought."

"Do you think anyone in Scottsbluff will remember me? Why would they?" I said before Abby could answer. "I haven't been back since I was eighteen."

"Not even for a high school reunion?"

"Nope."

"Didn't you have any friends you kept in touch with over the years?" Abby turned in her seat to face me.

"I had one friend I wrote letters to now and then. But after I got orders for overseas, I lost touch with her. Mail was notoriously slow. Remember, we're talking pre-computer days. Back then, snail mail or expensive long-distance calls were the only options for staying connected."

"Maybe you can look her up while we're there." Abby turned her attention to the scenery, and we drove in silence for the next several hours. Before merging onto I-80 in Lincoln, we stopped for a late breakfast and another cup of coffee to go.

"It's six hours from here to Scottsbluff. Let me know if you need to stop," I told Abby as we settled ourselves into the car again.

"*If* I need to stop? Yeah, I'll at least need a bathroom break. Won't you?"

"Probably, with all the coffee I'm drinking. Jen's told me I drive hard. I guess that means I don't stop a lot. Probably a holdover from my Marine Corps days."

"I think you drive *yourself* pretty hard."

"I never thought about that, but I suspect you're right. Does that mean more refining is on the agenda? The next ten weeks are stacking up to be pretty interesting." I chuckled. "After that big breakfast, I probably won't get hungry till supper time. Say the word and I'll stop whenever and for whatever."

"And if you want me to do some driving, just say so." Abby flashed me a smile, then settled deeper into her seat. Thirty minutes later I heard her softly snoring.

The miles and time whizzed by. Three hours later, Abby woke up and we pulled off for a pit stop.

"Before I dropped off to sleep, I was wondering. Did you happen to notify the local paper about your father's death?"

"That never even occurred to me." My stomach flip flopped and began to burn. "The man doesn't deserve an obituary."

"Everybody deserves an obituary. I'm sure he had friends who'd like to know he's died."

"Isn't it too late for an obit now? The funeral is tomorrow."

"That doesn't matter. A notice of death with his name, date of death, and where he's interred is plenty."

"He's been in prison for over twenty-five years. If he had any friends, they've probably forgotten about him." I stepped out of the car. While I filled the gas tank, Abby made a trip inside, returning with a bottle of water and a candy bar. I gathered our empty coffee cups from the console, tossed them into the trash, and made my way inside. I needed some chocolate.

As I returned to the car, Abby scrutinized me.

"Why are you so upset? You look like a grizzly stung by bees in his attempt to enjoy some honey."

"Have you seen your share of bears in Montana?" I started the car and pulled out.

"I have."

"I'm angry but not at you, Abby."

"I know. You're angry at your father. And you're filled with bitterness."

I hit my left turn signal and prepared to merge into the I-80 traffic.

"Sally, you've got to forgive him."

I took a deep breath and blew it out. "I have, over and over, but my emotions just never line up with my decision. I know God commands us to forgive. I…I just can't seem to let go of it."

"There's your problem. Forgiveness is a release of debt. It isn't based on feeling. Surely you know that."

I glanced at her, then shifted my focus back to the road. "Yes, I do."

"So, what are you not letting go of?"

"All the hurtful things he said and did. I had nightmares for years."

"That's what's allowed that bitterness to grow. Maybe while you're in Great Falls, you can take the time to work through it."

I sighed. "Maybe."

We settled into another comfortable silence as we sped down the interstate. I shoved the thoughts of my father to the back burner, turned to my current dilemma, and had a private conversation with the Lord as I jockeyed with the truck traffic.

Father, as You so often do, You answered one question before I even asked—I'm headed to Great Falls. As for this refining Abby's mentioned, I'm not sure I'm ready for it. You brought this life-changing inheritance of money and a ranch to me for a purpose. Help me be a good steward of it by showing me at least some of what You have planned.

Be patient, My daughter, one day at a time I will guide you along the best pathway for your life. Unfailing love surrounds those who trust Me.

After nearly eleven hours on the road, I pulled into the parking lot of a motel in Scottsbluff, and we dragged our tired carcasses inside. We checked in, took our bags to the room, then strolled across the street to a restaurant for supper.

"Eat hearty. We have a long day tomorrow." I perused the menu.

"The funeral isn't until ten o' clock, and have you forgotten you have to track down Mr. Schwartz? Don't be such a slave driver. We're in no rush to get to Great Falls." Abby smiled. "I know you're in a bad place right now. You're grieving and confused about what God has for you. But this goes much deeper. Your drive, your hardness, they're part of a wall you've constructed to keep yourself safe. It's got you in a prison as much as, if not more than, your father was."

I propped my elbows on the table and rested my chin in my hands. I stared questioningly over at Abby and felt tears welling in my eyes and choking my throat. Abby gave a half-hearted smile.

"Refining can be painful. Metals are refined by fire. Diamonds created by pressure. Pearls begin as a speck of sand. God's sanding off your hard edges."

"It makes me feel like I'm not good enough for Him, the same way my earthly father always made me feel." I felt a tear trickle down my cheek. I wiped it away. I hated crying.

"Oh, Sally, that's not it at all. God loves you, remember? He gave everything for you. He knows that hardness is hurting you. For one, it constantly blocks His love for you."

I lifted my head and straightened in my chair. "That hardness has helped me survive."

"Yes, it probably served you well while you were in the service, but it's long past time to let it go. You can't thrive and enjoy what God has for you if you're always focused on surviving."

A slim waitress approached our table, interrupting our conversation. Wrinkles of someone my age lined her face, and a few tresses of red streaked her gray hair.

"Hi, I'm Sarah. I'll be serving you tonight. Are you ready to order?" she asked, her pencil poised over her pad.

"*I* am. Are you, Sally?"

"Not quite. But you go ahead."

The waitress looked at me, then at Abby, then back at me.

"Not every day I see identical twins. You new in town or just visiting?" she asked.

"Just visiting." Abby handed the waitress her menu. "I'll have the Cobb salad and a cup of hot tea."

"Water for me, and the beef stew."

She wrote down my order, stared at me for several seconds, smiled pleasantly, then left.

I leaned across the table toward Abby as far as I could get and whispered, "Why was she staring at me like that?"

Abby shrugged and shook her head.

"I mean, why me and not you? We look alike."

"Except for our hair." Abby laughed. "You wear yours pretty short."

I watched the waitress fix Abby's cup of tea and my glass of water. She continued to stare at me as she returned to our table with our drinks.

"Is there some particular reason you keep staring at me?" I asked her.

She nearly dropped Abby's tea. "I'm so sorry. I didn't mean to. But you look so familiar. I went to high school with a girl named Sally. The only Sally I've ever known."

"How did you know my name is Sally?"

"Because your sister said it as I was taking your order."

"Oh. Guess I missed that. Sorry. I did grow up here, but I left after graduating from high school. That was forty years ago."

"Hmm, right time frame. But the Sally I knew didn't have a sister, let alone a *twin* sister."

A bell dinged from the kitchen and the cook yelled, "Order up."

The waitress looked back at the kitchen. "I'd better get back to work." She dashed off.

"How odd was that?" I said, astonished.

"Sally, this is a God appointment. She's probably someone you went to school with. Who was that friend you kept in touch with for a while?"

"Sarah Randall. And what do you mean, a God appointment?"

"A meeting God has specifically arranged. Sally, the waitress's name is Sarah."

My eyes popped open and I searched the room for her. She was busy serving another table. If that was Sarah Randall, she had changed a lot. Of course, most people do over the course of forty years.

"Getting back to our conversation." Abby drew my attention back to her. "Let's have some fun on this trip. It's nearly eleven hours to drive to Great Falls from here, and that's without stopping. We're in no rush. Let's visit some spots on the way, smell the roses as it were."

A thought struck me at Abby's words. "I hadn't realized it until now, but I've lost my joy. I rarely make time for fun."

"That's your hardness getting in the way."

I grimaced at her. "Okay, point taken. You have my permission to smack me when my hardness rears its ugly head."

"No way. I might nudge you softly." She grinned. "I'll let the Holy Spirit spar with you. He's better than I could ever be at sanding off rough edges."

We laughed together for a moment. Then while we waited for our food, Abby pulled up Google maps on her phone, and we studied possible places we could visit after our business in Scottsbluff. Finding Mr. Schwartz might prove elusive.

When Sarah brought our food, I asked, "Are you Sarah Randall?"

"Used to be. I've been Sarah O'Neil for the last thirty-five years. You're Sally Clark, aren't you?"

"Yes." I stood and hugged her. "You've changed so much I didn't recognize you."

"You've barely changed at all. But you never had a sister, and this lady could be your twin."

"She *is* my twin. Remember, I was adopted. Abby and I learned about each other this year, back in August."

"Wow! How fun. We need to catch up. I'm off tomorrow. How about breakfast here at eight?" Sarah always had been a take-charge kind of person.

"Is that okay with you, Abby? You'll join us, right?"

"I'd love to. It'll give me a chance to learn more about you."

"It's a date, Sarah. But we'll have to keep an eye on the time. I have to be at my father's funeral at ten."

"I'm sorry to hear that." Sarah gave me a brief hug. "I'll let Mom know. She was such good friends with your mom that I expect she'll want to honor her memory by attending your father's funeral."

"Can your mom join us for breakfast?" Abby asked.

"Probably. She owns and runs the diner, but our morning rush is usually over by 7:30."

"She must be in her late seventies by now, and she's running the diner?"

"Oh, yeah. She's a tough old bird as Dad would say. She's still going strong."

I gave Sarah another hug and sat down to my beef stew. Sarah returned to her work.

"Abby, why did you ask about her mother joining us?"

"Because she'll have memories of your life outside of your perspective. She'll know things you had no way of knowing as a child. Maybe even some insights into your father."

"Oh, you are devious." I gave her a sly smile. "Just don't get too nosy, okay?"

"I'm making no promises." A conspiratorial glint brightened her eyes.

###

That night my thoughts chased away any chance at sleep. Abby's rhythmic breathing in the next bed told me she was either too tired or unconcerned about things to have the same difficulty.

What were the odds of running into Sarah after being gone for forty years? No wonder Abby called it a God appointment. Only God could have arranged it. Who else might I run into while I was here in Scottsbluff? Would there be anyone at my father's funeral tomorrow? Maybe the funeral home had posted a death notice after all. My mind was in such a state of shock when I spoke to the funeral director several days ago that I honestly couldn't remember what I had agreed to.

Memories of school, of my father, of Mom rampaged through my mind. Why had I stayed angry at him all these years? I lay quietly, searching for an answer within myself and it came to me.

My anger gave me an excuse not to love him. If *he* didn't love *me*, why should I love *him*? I sensed an immediate conviction from the Holy Spirit about my attitude, so I opened the Bible app on my phone and read through several psalms to quiet my mind and calm my frustration.

I don't know at what point I fell asleep, but morning dawned much too soon. Thinking about breakfast with Sarah perked me up. Abby was already in the shower. I dragged myself out of bed and brewed a cup of coffee while I waited for my turn in the bathroom.

"Hey, sleepyhead," Abby said as she entered the room. "I thought you'd be up long before me. You usually are. You'd better hurry and get ready or we'll be late for breakfast."

###

"That's so amazing how you two discovered each other!" Sarah sat back in her chair as she took in our story. "A couple you met in Paris more than twenty years ago turns out to be the adoptive parents of your twin sister. Mom has *got* to hear this."

"I thought she was going to join us," I said.

"It's been an extra busy morning, but I think I can drag her away from the grill now." Sarah rose from her chair and walked to the back of the restaurant.

I took a bite of my hash browns and sausage while Abby devoured the pancakes she had smothered in blueberry syrup.

"Mom'll be out in a minute." Sarah took her seat again. "You remember she and your mom were best friends, don't you?"

"No, I don't remember that," I said, surprised. "It was all so long ago, and things with my father got so bad I guess that wiped out all the good. I do remember the time I spent at your house. Your family helped bring some sanity to my life. Did I ever say thank you?" I reached out and squeezed her hand.

Sarah smiled. "Not in so many words, but we knew."

Sarah's mom emerged from the swinging kitchen door, a pot of coffee in hand, and made her way to the table. She wore a white dress with large yellow sunflowers printed on it. A memory of my time at their house flashed before my eyes. Sunflowers everywhere! Her clothing, the upholstery, and a large garden of them in their backyard. She looked nearly the same as I remembered. Her hair had grayed and more wrinkles populated her face. Sarah and her mom looked so much alike. I stood and hugged her.

"Mrs. Randall, it's so good to see you. You've barely changed at all."

"Thank you, dear. And call me Ellen. I was so surprised last night when Sarah told me you were in town for your dad's funeral."

I sat as Mrs. Randall refilled all our cups, set the pot in the middle of the table, then sat in the chair next to Sarah. We chit-chatted about my time in the Marine Corps and my career as an editor. Sarah made me retell the story of how God brought Abby and me together, and Mrs. Randall was as astonished as Sarah had been.

"Isn't God so good?" Mrs. Randall said.

"Yes, He is." Abby pushed her now-empty plate to the side. "Since you and Sally's mom were good friends maybe you can tell us some things about Sally that she doesn't remember or never knew."

I directed a what-are-you-doing look at Abby.

"I'd be delighted to. What would you like to know?"

"What was she like as a little girl?" Abby asked.

Mrs. Randall laughed. "A pistol. Never sat still, climbed all the trees in her yard, scoured the neighborhood solving pretend mysteries. Being an MP in the Marines was a good fit for you."

"I remember climbing trees. Mom hated that. But I'd forgotten about the pretend mysteries." I gazed at Mrs. Randall and wondered if I could be brave enough to ask what I really wanted to know.

"What is it, Sally? Your eyes are filled with question." Mrs. Randall leaned forward. "Ask away."

I hesitated and took a gulp of coffee. Everyone at the table sat staring at me.

"You know how my father treated me after Mom died. How did she ever talk him into adopting me in the first place?"

"True, he wasn't one for kids, but he wanted your mom to be happy. You know, I…your mom…she…" Mrs. Randall stuttered and her face turned red.

"What is it, Mom? Are you okay?" Sarah leaned toward her mom, her arm going up around her mother's shoulders. Sarah frowned and her brow wrinkled. I guess she was as concerned as I was that something was physically wrong.

"I'm fine, Sarah. Don't worry. I'm just not sure if I should say what's on my mind. Helen made me promise never to say anything. But, Sally, now that your father is dead…"

I sat with bated breath, waiting to hear what weighed so heavily on Mrs. Randall's mind. It appeared everyone else was as well.

"Helen struggled with the guilt of it every day. I think it's partly what carried her to the grave so early."

"Mom," Sarah said. "You've got me on pins and needles here. Can you be any less cryptic? *I'm* frustrated wondering what it is. I can't imagine how Sally feels."

"I'm trying to picture my mom doing anything she'd feel guilty about," I said. "What did she do? And how does my father fit into this?"

"You're right, Sarah. I'm sorry, Sally." Mrs. Randall turned in her chair and reached out to grasp both my hands. "Your mother wanted to adopt you *and* your siblings." She glanced over at Abby. "But your father refused. It was one or none."

"Siblings?" Abby stressed the last *s*. Her eyes were so wide she looked like an owl, and the color had drained from her face. "How many of us were there?"

"There were three of you."

I dropped back in my chair, stunned. Mrs. Randall released my hands and continued. "Your mother made the choice of which one by saying eeny, meeny, miny mo. You two have a brother three years older than you."

This was no drop-my-coffee-cup moment like I had when I discovered I had a twin. This wasn't even a drop-the-whole-pot moment.

An exploding IED wouldn't have surprised me more.

Chapter Four

"Every good thing I have comes from you." Psalm 16:2b NLT

A brother! Abby and I had a brother! Abby's gaping mouth and owlish eyes reflected my own surprise at this news. I grabbed Abby's hand.

"Mrs. Randall, I...I...What orphanage did Mom adopt us from?"

"Oh, goodness, I don't remember the name of it. It closed down about twenty years ago and was converted to an apartment building."

"What a bombshell!" I released Abby's hand and worked to calm my mind.

"Sally, didn't you tell me last night your father's funeral was this morning?" Sarah asked.

Her question brought me out of my shock. I glanced at my phone for the time. "Yes. We've got to leave now if we're to get there on time. Would you two like to join us? It's not like there's going to be any service. The funeral director will say a few short words at the graveside and put the casket in the ground."

"What a sad commentary on one man's life." Mrs. Randall sighed. "Your father was a good man once. When your mom died, he did too. Of course, we'll come."

"We just need to pay our bill and we can go." Abby grabbing her purse from the floor.

"Breakfast is on the house," Mrs. Randall said. We all rose from our chairs. "What cemetery is it at?"

"Fairview," I told her. "We'll meet you there. And thank you for breakfast." I grabbed and hugged her tightly. "Thank you so much for telling us about Mom and about our brother."

We made our way to our cars and then to Fairview Cemetery. The drive only took ten minutes. Except for the surrounding rock bluffs, nothing about Scottsbluff looked familiar. Still, the town was clean and the air refreshing. Certainly not the hubbub and chaos of Kansas City.

When I pulled into the Fairview parking lot, a man at the entrance gave me directions to my father's grave site. I followed the road he directed me to, Mrs. Randall and Sarah directly behind us. As I rounded a curve, I spotted a canopy shading a prepared grave and a row of chairs. On the side of the lane was a hearse with two black-suited men standing next to it. No doubt funeral home staff.

A mustard yellow four-door sedan sat parked in front of the hearse. Chase leaned against the left front fender, looking like the well-muscled cowboy he was, dressed in a black western suit, white shirt, bolo tie, and boots. His black Stetson, the crowning piece to his outfit, shielded his eyes from the glimmering morning sun. His brightness in the sun forced me to recall the crunchy Cheeto image of him awash in the orange hue of sunset my first night at his ranch. I half-smiled at the memory.

"What is Chase doing here? Did you tell him about the funeral?"

"Of course I told him, but I didn't tell him to come."

Chase headed toward us while I parked several yards behind the hearse. I bolted from my seat. "Chase, *what* are you doing here?"

"Sally, I'm so sorry about your father." His arms rose as though he planned to hug me.

I jerked my hand up, palm out. A retort sat ready on my tongue. Why did I have only snarky words for Chase? Abby's warm hand on my back prevailed and I swallowed it instead. "Thank you, but you needn't have come such a long way for a fifteen-minute service."

"It was less than two hours flying time, and I wanted to be here for you."

"Why? I'm not grieving his loss. I hated the man."

Mrs. Randall's and Sarah's approach thwarted any response Chase might have had.

"Mrs. Randall, Sarah, this is my brother, Chase," Abby said. Chase removed his Stetson and nodded to each of them. He smoothed back his peppered gray hair and replaced the hat.

"My friends from childhood," I explained to Chase.

The two suited men approached me. "Ma'am, are you ready? If so, we'll place your father's casket."

"Yes, let's get this over with." I walked off.

"What burr got under her saddle?" I heard Chase ask.

"I expect the anger she buried forty years ago has risen from the grave," Abby answered.

Buried anger? If I gave that any amount of thought, I might find time to disagree with it. I shoved the comment away and took a seat in one the four available chairs.

Mom's grave was right next to my father's. A flood of memories ambushed me as I read her gravestone. *Much beloved wife and mother.* Death is hard for a ten-year-old to grasp. I remembered feeling so alone, but I also remembered Mrs. Randall. I smiled. She had stepped into Mom's shoes and mothered me. I didn't make it easy. I was too caught up in surviving my father to realize all the times Mrs. Randall was there for me. Now, I did.

She was with me the day I stood before the judge on my third shoplifting charge and asked him why I couldn't have the choices of the military or jail like he'd given someone else. As shocked as the judge's face looked concerning my question, I wonder what Mrs. Randall's had looked like.

"Are you ready for the service, Miss Clark?" The funeral director drew my attention back to the here and now. I looked around at the gathering. Only five of us. Abby, Sarah, and Mrs. Randall had taken the other three available seats. Chase stood off to the left.

"Yes, please begin."

The only part of the director's message that caught my attention was that he had known my father. Chase's presence and Mrs. Randall's revelation about my brother occupied my thoughts. The service was brief, as I suspected it would be. The funeral director moved out from under the canopy. Chase moved to stand in from of me.

"Would you give me a minute to say goodbye?" I looked at Chase, then at Abby, Sarah, and Mrs. Randall.

They nodded and headed toward the cars, but not without each of them first giving me a hug.

I approached the casket. "Father, I can't believe you forced Mom to choose one out of the three of us. Just one more thing I need to forgive. You've left the misery of this life behind, but did you trade it for something even worse? As angry as I am at you…I guess I must have loved you once because I cringe to think of you being in hell." I took a long slow breath and blew it out just as slowly. "Goodbye."

I stepped over to my mom's grave. "Mom, he's gone, but you probably know that. I…how…why couldn't it have been him all those years ago instead of you? He…" A few hot tears trickled down the side of my nose on its journey to my lips. I licked them away. Tasting their saltiness reminded me of the tang of my life. "I love you, Mom. I miss you."

I dried my tears and returned to my car where Chase, Abby, Sarah, and Mrs. Randall stood chatting. "Thanks for waiting. Mrs. Randall, I have so much to thank you for, and I should have said it long before now. Your family and home gave me a safe place to be when I was a teen. I didn't realize it then, but I do now. You, Mr. Randall, and Sarah kept me out of a lot of trouble."

"It was our pleasure, Sally. I loved your mother. She was my dearest friend. When she was diagnosed as terminal, she asked me to look after you. So as I see it, I was just fulfilling my promise to her. She'd be very proud of the woman you've become." Her eyes glistened, and my tears threatened to return.

"Thank you for telling me that. And thank you for looking after me. Sarah, what's your phone number and email address? I want to keep in touch." I entered her info into my phone as she spoke.

"How long are you here in town, Sally?" Mrs. Randall asked.

"Not really sure. Apparently Father had a will. I need to find his lawyer, Mr. Schwartz."

"Kurt Schwartz?" Mrs. Randall asked.

"Yes. Do you know him?" Abby said.

"I did. He died several years ago. Let me think a minute."

While Mrs. Randall searched her memory, I turned my face up to the sun and soaked in its warmth and calming energy, then swiped at a few tears that had escaped.

"Steinbeck and Steinbeck," she blurted. "That's the law firm he was with."

"That's a big help." I squeezed her hands. "I'll start there. Thank you."

"Why don't you three join me and my family for dinner tonight? Say, seven o' clock?" Sarah suggested.

"I'm sure Chase needs to get back to Montana." I glared at him. Would he get the message that I didn't want him here?

"No, I don't." He glared back at me. "I'd like to join you, thank you."

"When are you planning on leaving, Chase?" I gritted my teeth. "I'm sure Abby will want to join you."

"Are you kidding?" Abby scoffed. "I'm not leaving you here alone to figure out this mess. Are you forgetting about the brother we need to find?"

"Brother?" Chase's eyebrows shot up and his eyes widened.

"Yes, Sally and I have a brother! I'll tell you all about it back at the motel."

"Well then, I think that's settled," Sarah said. "I'll see you all at my house for dinner. I'll text you the address, Sally. See you at seven." She and Mrs. Randall got into her car.

I watched them drive away while Abby gave Chase directions to the hotel. So much for getting rid of Chase.

Men. They were only kind when they wanted something from you.

###

"I've got enough adrenaline coursing through me to animate a mummy." I plopped down on the hotel bed, kicked off my black pumps, and stretched my toes. I hadn't worn these shoes since I'd attended Mr. Pendrake's funeral back in March, and I was more than ready to get out of my black dress and pantyhose and into something more comfortable. "I'd better get changed before Chase gets here."

"There's no rush. He didn't have any breakfast and said he was going to stop for a bite before meeting us here."

"All the same. Why did he have to come? I have enough to occupy my mind without having to deal with him."

"Sally, I've never seen you this prickly before. Did you eat cactus for breakfast?"

"Very funny." I rose from the bed and jerked a pair of jeans and a red, black, and white plaid shirt out of my suitcase.

"I'm serious." Abby grabbed my shoulders and turned me to face her. "You've been hotheaded since you got the call about your father. He hurt you deeply, and his death has ripped the scab off that wound. Now the ugly infection that's festered for forty years is spewing out onto everyone around you."

I stood staring at her. Could what she said be true?

"What do you do when you need to clear your head?"

"I usually go for a walk or a run."

"Then I highly recommend you do." Abby nodded as she spoke. "There's plenty of time before Chase gets here. And if you're not back by then, I'll update him about our brother."

"Okay." I sighed. She let go of my shoulders and went over to her suitcase. I draped my jeans and shirt across the back of my suitcase and rummaged for my running gear. "I think a run will do me the best. I'll be at least a half hour."

"Take all the time you need." Abby raised her eyebrows at me.

"I'm sorry I've been such a grouch."

I changed into my running clothes and stepped outside to survey the area for a possible running route. Nothing but businesses to the east and no sidewalk. South appeared to head out of town. I set off on the road, facing the traffic.

I did need to clear my head, but I also needed to think. There was an oxymoron in there somewhere. Being in the middle of enemy fire seemed less dangerous than facing Chase.

When I returned to my room, a full hour had passed. Chase and Abby sat at the round table the small room afforded.

"So, Chase, how long were you planning on being here?" I grabbed a towel from the bathroom and approached the table while I wiped the sweat from my face.

"Sally!" Abby reproached.

"What? I didn't mean here in our room. I meant in Scottsbluff. Have you had a chance to update him?"

Chase gave me a wry smile. "I had planned to fly home tonight after dinner with you and the O'Neils. But with this news of a brother, maybe I can stay and help."

I shrugged. "Don't know how you could. We only just found out ourselves this morning."

"We were discussing that when you came in," Abby said.

"Oh, okay. Continue. I need a shower. You can fill me in on what you've come up with when I get done." I grabbed my clothes and zipped into the bathroom. When I emerged fifteen minutes later, Chase and Abby were hard at work. I dug my tablet from the suitcase and joined them.

"Thoughts are pinging around in my head like a pinball on steroids. I guess the first place to start is to see what I can find out at Steinbeck and Steinbeck about my father's will, but I'd really rather find out about our brother."

"I already called Steinbeck and Steinbeck," Abby said. "You have an appointment tomorrow at nine with Mr. Brown, who took over Mr. Schwartz's clients after he died."

"Okay. Thanks. What else did you accomplish while I was out running?"

"That's all. I think the next step is to find out the name of the orphanage."

"I bet Karl would have that," Chase said.

"Karl?"

"Our lawyer in Great Falls, remember?" Abby said.

"Oh, yeah. Why would he have that information?"

"For one, I expect that's where Pop adopted Abby from, and two, because Pop had him do some research on you when he and Mom returned from Paris," Chase said.

They researched me? My stomach somersaulted. "It's unnerving to know he did that. Makes me feel like I'm some criminal or something."

"Sally, that's not it at all," Abby said.

"I know they had to investigate things, but it doesn't stop the Devil from regularly slinging accusations my way." After all, how else would they find out anything about me? The ping pong balls in my head were interfering with my rational thought.

"Pop said in his video he would have adopted you had he known about you when he adopted me. That means our brother got adopted before I did."

"At the very least, Karl should have the name of the orphanage and would know the right channels to ask for records," Chase said. "Maybe he has the names of your birth parents."

"Do you think we could find them too?" I asked.

"They're dead. Karl told me that much when he told me I was adopted."

"Dead? I…I didn't know that." I dropped back in my chair, a bit of my energy dissipating.

"I'm sorry. I guess I assumed you knew," Abby said.

"No. I've always figured my biological mother gave me up for some reason or another. Did Karl tell you anything more than that?"

"No. Since there were three of us at the orphanage, it's probably a safe assumption that our parents died at the same time in a car crash or something similar."

I sat contemplating that thought for a moment. "There have to be birth records somewhere for us, doesn't there? I'd like to know more about my real family, wouldn't you?"

"Yeah. I expect that desire is stronger for you having grown up with your father's rejection." Abby turned to Chase. "Do you have Karl's number in your phone? I don't."

"Yeah, I've got it."

He dialed, put the phone on speaker, and laid it in the middle of the table.

"Kandell Law Offices, how may I help you?"

"Cindy, this is Chase Reynolds. Is Karl available?"

"He's in court today, Chase. Would you like to leave a message?"

"Maybe you can help. We need to find out the name of the orphanage where Pop adopted Abby. It should be in the file he has on Sally Clark."

"I have a brief I need to get ready, but I'll see what I can find and call you back. Will that work?"

"Sure. Thank you, Cindy. I appreciate it." Chase clicked off the call and turned to me. "Looks like we're in for a waiting game. First one inheritance and now another. Are you wondering what your father's will might hold?"

"I...I hadn't given it much thought beyond the house we lived in. Do I need to bring anything with me tomorrow for the appointment with the lawyer?"

"He wanted a death certificate. I already called the funeral home to see what they could provide," Chase explained.

"Thank you. What's next?"

"Finding your brother." Chase looked at me then at Abby. "Surely there are adoption papers on file for each of you. I expect there'd be some at the county or state courthouse."

The thought struck me that I might not even be in my father's will. Not that it mattered; his last will and testament had to be executed. The fact that he had one meant he had personal property of some kind that he wanted someone to have.

"Chase, I forgot to tell you. I invited Sally to spend Thanksgiving through New Year's with me and she agreed."

"You actually agreed to that?" Chase's eyes were wide and a chuckle escaped. "Are you sure? Abby didn't twist your arm or anything?"

I laughed. "No, she didn't twist my arm. My plan to buy the publishing company I used to work for fell through. Abby suggested some time in Montana might be helpful for me to seek God's direction."

"When are you coming and how do you plan to get there? Should I let Steve know to plan a flight?"

"No need," Abby said, "we planned to head there when we got done here in Scottsbluff."

"But Thanksgiving's a month away. Don't you need time to grieve?"

"I'm fine. I suppose that's because the Marine in me says 'suck it up and move on.'"

"You need to allow yourself to grieve your father's loss," Chase said.

"That's what I told her." Abby shook her head. "I'm still marveling that she agreed to come to Great Falls."

I expect Chase was marveling at that fact too. I honestly never expected to return to Montana. Could you blame me? Their ranch foreman had tried to kill me. If I was dead, my share of the inheritance would revert to his wife, Chase's daughter. To compound the situation, Chase told me he was falling in love with me—that scared me more than the three attempts to kill me. As a Marine, facing death was old hat.

"Are you planning on taking off work during Sally's visit? How will she keep herself entertained if you're at work all week long?"

"She's a big girl. She can play tourist and visit all the places she didn't get to see back in August. I'm sure those nephews of mine can easily talk her into working with the horses again." Abby chuckled. "Actually, the horses convinced her into coming."

"If you work with the horses, Sally, you might as well stay at the ranch."

"I see that glint in your eye, Chase," Abby said. "You're excited. You'd rather she stay at the ranch."

"Abby, don't be ridiculous. You make me sound like some lovestruck teenager."

I looked at Abby and half frowned, half smiled.

"How 'bout we play things by ear? Sally, you decide where you want to stay," Chase suggested.

"Sounds like a plan," I said. "I'm looking forward to enjoying your housekeeper's great cooking."

Shocking news seemed to be the soup *du jour*. First, my buy-out offer gets turned down, then my father dies, then I learn I have a brother. What other shocking news might be barreling my way?

"Now I understand how you felt, Sally, when you saw what you thought was a picture of you on the dining room wall. And, Abby, how you must have felt when Karl told us you were adopted. I'm so sorry for not fully grasping how all this has impacted you two. But surely you're excited about having a brother?"

"Definitely. We both are," Abby said. "Since we're in a holding pattern, I think I'll see what I can find at the courthouse with a search of birth records."

"But how would you know where to start?" Chase's eyebrows creased along with his frown. "You don't even have a last name."

"Mrs. Randall said our brother was three years older, so I can start by looking at the births for that year. I know it's probably hard for you to understand, Chase—"

"I understand perfectly. Of course you want to find your brother. I'll do whatever I can to help."

"That would be wonderful," Abby said.

"Chase, are you sure my prolonged visit won't disrupt things at the ranch?"

"Not at all, Sally. And I'm sure the boys would love having you there."

"Okay, as long as you're sure."

"I'm sure." He nodded as if to add conviction to his words.

"I'd say the ball is well and truly rolling," Abby said.

"Agreed." My stomach rumbled, telling me it was nearly noon. I called the funeral home about the paperwork Mr. Brown needed. They said they'd already faxed it over. That would save me the trip over there, and I'd be able to join Abby and Chase in the search of birth records.

We dashed across the street to Mrs. Randall's diner for a quick lunch.

"Where can we find the county courthouse?" Abby asked the clerk as we paid our bill.

"That's down in Gering."

"How far is that from here?" I asked.

The clerk shrugged. "Not sure, ten minutes maybe, at the most. It's south of the river."

"Okay, thanks." I took my receipt and credit card and put them in my purse. The three of us made our way across the street to my car in the hotel parking lot. "I'll look it up on Google maps."

Fifteen minutes later we pulled up to the Scotts Bluff County Courthouse. The moment I climbed out of the car and stood looking at the building, memories came rushing back. The building had not only claimed its place on the National Register of Historic Places, but had also claimed its place in *my* history.

"Sally, are you okay?" Chase asked.

His question brought me out of my reverie. "Yeah, I'm fine. I was just remembering. It didn't click before, but I stood before a judge in this building three times as a teenager."

The trees had grown considerably in the last forty years, obscuring much of the front of the building. Its neoclassical architecture reminded me of the many US government buildings I'd been in over the years—especially post offices—with its yellow brick construction and six white columns that stood tall and distinctive. As we approached the east entrance, I leaned my head back to look at the clock at the top of the four-story structure.

"How would my life have turned out if the judge had insisted on sending me to jail rather than allowing me to join the military?"

"Only God knows the answer to that," Abby said.

We crossed the street and made our way into the building. We scanned the directory, then approached the deputy standing guard. We plopped our things in a plastic bucket so they could be scanned and made our way through the metal detector. Then, reclaiming our things, we headed to the clerk's office.

We only waited in line ten minutes. Chase took a seat along the wall.

"How can I help you ladies?" the gentleman behind the counter asked.

"I expect you hear this often enough. We were orphaned as children and adopted by different families. We learned this morning that we have a brother. All we have to go on is his year of birth. Would it be possible to search the birth records?"

"You'll have to contact the state's vital records office. Let me give you their number." He jotted down the phone number on a piece of paper and handed it to me.

"Thank you." I took the paper, and we made our way back out to the car. "Well, that didn't get us very far."

"At least we know what office to contact. Let's find the library and see if they have digitized copies of the newspaper for that year. We can see if there were any birth announcements."

"Great idea, Abby! Here, take my keys. I'll zip inside and ask the deputy if he knows the address for the library, then meet you at the car."

In short order we parked at the library and made our way inside. The clerk was quite friendly and got us set up with what we needed.

"I'll take January through April. Abby, you take May through August, and Chase, September through December." And so our afternoon disappeared as we searched birth announcements. After four hours of searching and reading, we walked away with only ten names.

Chapter Five

"Yes, I have a good inheritance." Psalm 16:6b NKJV

Dinner with the O'Neils turned out to be a pleasant evening. Sarah, her husband, Barry, and I spent most of the evening reminiscing about our school days. Mr. and Mrs. Randall shared more memories of my parents and my childhood antics. And Abby and Chase soaked it all in. Before the evening was over, Mrs. Randall coaxed childhood memories out of Abby and Chase too.

"I'd better be getting to the airport," Chase said. "I told Steve to be ready to lift off by ten. Thank you for dinner, Sarah. It was nice meeting you and Barry."

We exchanged handshakes and hugs. Chase walked to his rental car, and Abby and I walked to my car.

"Text me when you get in," Abby told Chase.

"Sure thing, sis." Chase smiled. "And keep me updated on things."

Chase drove off and Abby and I, feeling like teenagers again, returned to the hotel.

I greeted Friday morning at my usual five a.m., having caught up on the sleep I'd lost the night before. Abby was still sound asleep, and I determined not to wake her. Excitement energized me. What shocking news might my nine o' clock meeting with the lawyer bring?

I checked the weather app on my phone for the temperature. A crispy 44 degrees, too chilly to sit outside for my quiet time with God. I peeked out the curtains. Though the sun wouldn't rise for several more hours, the nearly full moon bathed the landscape of bluffs outside my hotel window in an inviting soft white light. The hotel's complimentary breakfast wasn't available until six. I dressed, grabbed my Bible, and made my way to the lobby.

"Good morning," I said to the desk clerk.

"Good morning, ma'am," he replied. "The weather's promising another warmer than usual fall day."

I stopped to chat with him a bit. "You know, it's been hotter than usual where I live in Kansas City, too, all summer long and into the fall."

"I've often found that means a colder than usual winter."

"I hope not. I like snow, but I hate the cold that comes with it." I chuckled. "Have a nice day." I stepped outside for a full view of the pre-dawn sky. Stars galore with the waning moon beginning its descent. I drank in the sight. You couldn't get this in Kansas City. I had donned my favorite Nebraska Huskers sweatshirt, but I didn't tarry in the chilly air. I made my way back to the hotel lobby, got comfortable on one of the two sofas that furnished the area, and opened my Bible to the proverb of the day.

A wise woman builds her home, but a foolish woman tears it down with her own hands.

The verse jumped off the page at me. I couldn't read beyond verse one. I thought about my anger toward my father, boiling just below the surface, and Abby's reprimand yesterday about being so prickly. Was my anger tearing down my house?

Father, I don't know what all you have for me, but I know I need Your wisdom as I face each day. Thank You for providing guidance for my every step and decision. Help me and Abby find our brother.

###

"There you are." Abby's voice woke me.

Apparently, I had drifted off while bathed in that peace only God can give. I looked up. "Good morning. I didn't want to wake you so I came down here to read."

"You needn't have worried, but thank you. Are you hungry? I'm famished. Hotel breakfast or across the street to Mrs. Randall's diner?"

"Let's see what the hotel has to offer." We made our way down the hallway, the scents of freshly brewed coffee and bacon guiding us. The hotel put on a nice spread: waffles, biscuits, sausage gravy, bacon, scrambled eggs, fruit, cereal, and toast. "This looks great, and we have the room to ourselves right now."

We filled our plates and took a seat.

"You'll come with me to meet the lawyer today, right?" I asked.

"I don't know. Surely that's something private for you."

"Not at all. Besides, as emotionally sensitive as I am where my father is concerned, I might need your level head. God told me today that a wise woman builds her house, but a foolish one tears it down." I took a sip of my first coffee of the day, then tucked into my scrambled eggs and bacon.

"That does have a rather prophetic tone considering your current situation. If you really want me there, I'll go." Abby had opted for biscuits and gravy and an orange.

"Thanks, Abby. You've been such a big help, but I know I'm keeping you from work."

"Emily is managing just fine. And it's good experience for her without me or Leslie there to look over her shoulder."

We chatted for over an hour while we enjoyed our breakfast, then returned to the room. We passed the remaining hour before my appointment with Bible reading. The minutes agonizingly ticked by.

"How about after we see Mr. Brown, we start a search on the list of names we got from the library?" I suggested as we prepared to leave.

"Let's see what news your father's will might have before we make plans for the afternoon."

"I'm still flabbergasted that he even had a will."

The drive to Mr. Brown's office took about eight minutes in what I assumed was the Scottsbluff morning rush hour. Maybe their rush hour occurred earlier in the morning. Admittedly, even the traffic in Kansas City seemed mild compared to the chaos of cars I dealt with in Paris years ago, which was partly to blame for my dislike of traffic.

As I stood looking at the door to Steinbeck and Steinbeck, a swarm of butterflies invaded my stomach. I took a deep breath and plunged through the door. The receptionist sat at her desk and a man stood next to her giving her instructions on something he needed typed. He looked up from his task.

"Good morning. I'm Sally Clark. I have a nine o' clock with Mr. Brown."

"I'm Mark Brown. I didn't realize there were two of you."

"This is my sister, Abby. She's the one who called you yesterday. I'm not sure she mentioned that Sam Clark was my adoptive father. A different family adopted Abby."

"I'm sorry for your loss, Miss Clark. Mr. Schwartz died several years back and I took on his clients." He shook our hands in turn, finished his instructions with the receptionist, then ushered us into his office. "Please sit down."

We took a seat and I looked at him questioningly. He had the same sky blue eyes Abby and I had and a similar set to his chin. Wisps of gray at each temple shaded his distinctly blond hair. I estimated he was at least my age if not a little older. "Where do we start?"

"The funeral director faxed me the prison's death certificate on your father. If you like, I can order the official certificates you'll need for notifying other entities that need to be informed. The director assured me you are who you say you are. I would, however, like to make a copy of your driver's license for our records."

He waited while I dug it out of my wallet, then rose and left the office. I heard the hum of a copy machine, and then he returned, handing me my license as he strode past me and once again took a seat behind his desk. "After yesterday's call, I pulled your father's file and reviewed it. The executor is a Mr. Jeremiah Nathaniel. I'm not acquainted with him, but I have been able to get in touch with him and notified him of the death. He managed your father's assets while he was in prison."

"My father had assets?" I looked at Abby. "I didn't expect that. Does Mr. Nathaniel live locally?"

"Yes, he does. Apparently there are also some small personal items your father wanted distributed to relatives. Mr. Nathaniel has kept them safe. Your father has willed you 50 percent of his monetary assets, which aren't substantial, but neither are they meager. He also owned a house, which is all yours."

"How could he have financial assets? He was in prison for at least the last twenty-five years. I figured any money he had went to pay a lawyer for his trial."

"He rented out the home he owned, so he's had income from that. He also has a retirement account. I can give you the address for the house, but the Realtor who manages the property has the keys." He plucked a paper from the file on his desk and handed it to me. "Here's the address, the Realtor's name and number, and also Mr. Nathaniel's number. I'll be meeting with him later today to go over his duties. It's all quite straightforward actually, nothing complicated."

I took the paper from him and glanced at the information. I didn't recognize the address. "I…I'm so surprised. The man hated me. Why would he have willed me anything?"

"Hated you?" Mr. Brown said, leaning forward across his desk.

"Oh, long story." I waved my hand toward him. "He wasn't really one for kids."

"Obviously he didn't hate you," Abby said.

"Sir, we learned yesterday that we have a brother. Do your files contain any information on my adoption? We're trying to find out the name of the orphanage."

He flipped through the papers of his file, stopping briefly now and then to scan a page. "No, I don't see anything. I'm certain the state would have record of it. Would you like me to do a bit of research?"

"No, but thank you. We're waiting to hear back from my lawyer in Montana," Abby said. "And we've got a few other avenues we're utilizing in our search for our brother."

"I would like for you to file for the official death certificate, Mr. Brown. I have plenty of other things to occupy my time."

"How many would you like?"

"How many? Who all needs to know?"

"Life insurance companies, the government most certainly, the VA if he was military, any company that might hold a retirement account for him, and more. Ten copies is often the standard. Why don't you call me after you visit with Mr. Nathaniel and have a better idea of what you'll need. I'm certain the banks here in town accept copies of the certified original."

I rose from my chair and Abby followed suit.

Seemed it was the year for inheritances.

How many more surprises could my brain take in?

"What do we do first?" I punched my key fob and unlocked the doors while we approached the car.

"Let's just sit here in the car and think things through."

We eased into our seats, and I rolled the windows down to let the fresh air blow through. It was barely 9:30.

"Why don't you call the Realtor first and make an appointment, then call Mr. Nathaniel? As a friend of your father's, he's probably retired and more likely to be available to visit with you yet this morning."

"You're right. Why can't I think straight?"

Abby chortled. "Well, let's see. You just buried your father; you learned yesterday you have a brother; today you learned your father has willed you 50 percent of his financial assets and a house. You're overwhelmed with it all."

"I suppose. But it's not like I've never faced major stress before."

"But this stress is directly connected to your father and all the emotional baggage you carry."

"Humph, emotional baggage is right!" I pulled my phone from my pocket and made the necessary phone calls. The Realtor wasn't available until late this coming Monday afternoon. Mr. Nathaniel said, "come on over."

The drive to Mr. Nathaniel's was a short one. His yard burst with color, the trees reaching their fall majesty. Wine, yellow, and rust chrysanthemums in large pots dotted the front porch. Mr. and Mrs. Nathaniel sat in wicker chairs, enjoying the mild weather, or were they on the lookout for me? They were both gray-headed and bore the wrinkles of those in their late seventies. Abby and I exited the car.

"Good morning, Mr. Nathaniel," I said as we walked up the driveway. He rose from his chair.

"Good morning. Let's bypass the formalities. Call me Jeremiah and this is my wife, Claire." He pointed to her, then came down the porch steps, his hand extended. "I thought Sam only had one daughter?"

"He did. He was only willing to adopt one child, so my sister, Abby, and I got split up. How long did you know Father?"

He led the way back up the stairs and pointed us to the porch swing.

"Can I get you something to drink?" Claire asked.

"I'd love a cup of tea, if it's no trouble," Abby said.

"Coffee's fine for me. Black."

Claire got up and went into the house. I noticed an ashtray full of cigarette butts on the wicker table next to Mr. Nathaniel's chair. That would explain the raspy breath I'd noticed during our phone call. I looked at him, hopeful he hadn't forgotten my question.

"I've known Sam since we were in grade school. Even though I knew he had cancer, I'm still struggling to believe he's gone. I don't get the paper no more, so didn't know about the funeral. Otherwise I'd have been there."

"I'm not sure there was anything in the paper anyway," I said. "I can't remember if I had the funeral home submit anything."

There was an awkward silence between us while we waited for Claire to return.

"I meet with Mr. Brown this afternoon to go over yer dad's will. When he got sent to prison, he had me collect all his personal things and put them into storage. I expect I'll sell most of them, but there are a few he wanted given to some relatives and friends. He had hoped for an appeal to turn around his conviction." Jeremiah shrugged.

Claire returned with a tray laden with matching cups and saucers, along with cream and sugar dishes that matched the pattern on the cups. "Here we are." She held the tray out toward us.

"Thank you," Abby and I chimed while we grabbed our cups. Abby added a bit of sugar to her tea, then Claire laid the tray on the table next to Jeremiah.

Our conversation was stifled and awkward, and before long a chilly breeze whooshed across the yard, raining down a rainbow of leaves. I managed to learn my father had made a list of all his accounts after he was convicted and had given Jeremiah power of attorney over his affairs. Jeremiah had managed them all while my father was in prison.

"I expect you'll want to look at the house. It's quite nice," Jeremiah said.

"I've already made an appointment with the Realtor for Monday. I'll probably drive by and at least take a look from the outside." I rose and set my empty cup and saucer on the tray. "I guess we'd better be on our way. Thank you so much for your time."

"Let me get you that list of yer dad's accounts before you go." He quickly disappeared into the house, but it was several minutes before he returned. "I had to do some digging to find it. There's this too." He held out the list to me. I took a picture of it with my phone. He pulled an envelope from his pants pocket. "I got this in the mail about a year ago when he learned he had terminal cancer. Said to be sure you got it after he died."

I froze. All I could do was stare at that envelope.

"Thank you so much, Jeremiah. I'm sure we'll be in touch again before we leave town." Abby took the envelope. She grabbed my arm and propelled me toward the steps, bringing me to my senses.

"Yes, thank you. It was nice to meet you both." We made our way to the car. Abby handed me the envelope before I started the car. I took it and shoved it into my purse.

Was I ready to face whatever was in there?

Chapter Six

"Keep me safe, O God, for I have come to
you for refuge." Psalm 16:1 NLT

I think I've done all I can until Monday when I see the Realtor. What do we do between now and then?" I asked as we headed back to the hotel from Jeremiah's.

"Mt. Rushmore isn't far from here. Let's drive up to Rapid City and spend the weekend there, then come back Monday morning. Have you ever been there?"

"No, I haven't. I think that's a great idea. Hopefully, it'll give my brain a break." I glanced at the clock on the dash. "It's nearly checkout time at the hotel. We'd better step on it."

"I'll let the front desk know our plans on our way in and reserve a room for Monday."

In short order, I pulled into the hotel parking lot.

Twenty minutes later while I loaded the trunk, clouds shrouded the sun, and the wind had turned even colder. "That wind has gotten nasty. I'm getting my winter coat out of the suitcase."

"I didn't bring one, so a sweater and my jacket will have to do." Abby took a sweater from her suitcase and slipped it on over her shirt then pulled her jacket out from the bottom of the suitcase.

I quickly rummaged through my dress bag for my coat and hurried to the driver's seat. I tossed my coat in the backseat and grabbed my atlas, then settled myself behind the steering wheel. "I'm glad we've only got a short drive ahead of us. Fighting this wind will be tiring. I hope it isn't like this tomorrow while we're at Rushmore."

I studied the map and decided the scenic route through the Oglala National Grassland would be fun.

"Don't you want to just use GPS?" Abby asked.

"No, I much prefer to know what roads I need than wait for the GPS to tell me ten seconds before I need to turn. I did check Google maps to see how long it'll take. A little over three hours. We'll have time for sightseeing tonight once we get to Rapid City." I started the car, pulled out of the parking lot, and headed north on State Highway 71. "Who would have imagined that my father's death would lead to us discovering we have a brother?"

"Isn't God amazing?" Abby grabbed my arm resting on the stick shift. "Let's do one of those DNA tests like you can get through Ancestry.com or 23andMe. We might be able to find other relatives."

"A DNA test would give us conclusive proof we're sisters."

"Mrs. Randall did that. Do you have reason to doubt her word?"

"No, not at all. I guess I was thinking about Chase…and Leslie."

"My niece has changed a lot since you first met her. And Chase never cared about definitive proof. Neither did Pop. Are you forgetting Pop's last will and testament video? He might not have given you his last name, but giving you the inheritance was his way of adopting you."

"I'd forgotten that. Thanks for reminding me." I smiled at her. "You're so wise."

"Not me. God. I've spent my life reading the Bible and learning His wisdom." She repositioned herself in her seat. "Where's that atlas? I think I'll look at alternative routes to Great Falls."

I pulled the atlas from between the seat and the center console and handed it to her.

My excitement about having a brother conflicted with my anger toward my father and his refusal to adopt my siblings. How that burden must have weighed on Mom. Maybe Mrs. Randall was right about it sending Mom to an early death. Now confusion added itself to the emotions plaguing me. Father had included me in his will.

I shoved aside those emotions and my grief at what might have been and decided to enjoy the drive and the scenery while Abby studied the map. I had expected lots of trees, though I don't know why. Instead, mile after mile of hilly grassland spread out before us. Gray clouds colored it all a dull green, and the ocean of grass waved in the wild wind.

The first feathers of snow drifted across the windshield thirty minutes into the drive. Snow? How could that be? It was only mid-October.

"Abby, is that snow I'm seeing?" Yesterday's high was 70 degrees and the morning started at 44 degrees. I might have expected this in Montana, but I never gave it a thought for Nebraska. Abby looked up from the map and watched for a minute or so.

"I think it is. It's a minor flurry. No big deal."

But the farther north we drove, the heavier the snowfall grew. An hour or so later when we reached the Oglala Grassland, the snow had escalated to blizzard conditions. Fierce wind gusts pounded the car and blew the snow horizontally. Only the tall green grass along the roadside gave clues to the edge of the road.

The blizzard conditions forced my speed down to 35 mph and less. My hands ached from gripping the steering wheel against the buffeting wind. The wipers, running on high, failed to clear the snow from the windshield. Despite the heater blowing, also on high, I shivered from my toes up to my waist—nerves, most likely. But then again, all the heat was aimed at the windshield to melt the onslaught of snow. Still the snow accumulated under the wipers.

"I've got to clear the windshield." I stopped the car in the road, shifted into neutral, and set the brake. I reached down and tucked my jeans into my socks, then reached for my coat in the backseat and pulled it on.

"I'll get this side," Abby said, zipping her jacket.

"No way! You're not dressed for this. I am. Besides, there's no sense in both of us getting cold. I'll be fine. You just stay put." I dreaded getting out of the car, but I turned on the emergency flashers and stepped out.

The icy wind stripped the air from my lungs the moment I opened the door, leaving a burning sensation behind. I held my breath and jogged around to clear the passenger side first. I lifted the wiper and scooped the snow to the ground. Much of the slushy snow stuck to my gloves. That done, I rushed to the driver side and did the same.

When I climbed back into the car, I unzipped my coat enough to fold down the collar. Every muscle from my neck to my toes ached with tension. I took a deep breath and tried to relax as I exhaled. "We should have checked the weather forecast before we left the hotel." I settled into my seat and turned off the flashers, then shifted into first gear, and slowly started down the highway again, managing 30 mph in third gear. "We totally missed the warning signs."

"What warning signs?"

"That bitter north wind that blew in like a tornado and brought these leaden clouds. I never imagined snow this early in October. I hate the thought of stopping somewhere to wait it out. We're halfway there."

"Yes, but getting caught in a blizzard out on the highway doesn't thrill me."

"We're pretty much out in the middle of nowhere, and there's been no traffic in either direction. Check the map for the nearest town. I think we're nearly through the Grasslands."

Abby briefly studied the map. "The nearest place is a little town called Ardmore, right on the state line. Give me your phone."

"My phone?" I leaned over and reached back to my left pants pocket and pulled it out. "Here. Who you gonna call?"

"No one. I'm going to plug it in and use the GPS." She fumbled with the cord. "Drat. No signal." She grabbed her purse and pulled out her phone. "No signal on my phone either. Do you have OnStar?"

"No." I shivered. "It's like we're the only two people on the planet."

"Maybe we can get some news from the radio." Abby turned up the volume and hit the seek button several times.

"Flashlights, candles, hurricane lamps. Make sure you've got gas for your generator. This blizzard is expected to last the next thirty-six hours. This is KNEB Better Country 94.1 FM in Scottsbluff." A song came on and Abby turned the volume down.

"Let's pray." She didn't wait for me to stop the car. She snatched my hand off the stick shift just as I shifted into second gear and slowed to 25 mph. "God, we know You're our protector and provider. Bring an end to this storm or make it let up long enough to show us a safe haven."

"Amen."

I love you both, my two beautiful daughters. Of course I will provide for and protect you.

God's answer nearly brought me to tears. Until that point, I hadn't realized how on edge my nerves were, not just about the storm, but about everything happening in my life.

Thank you, Father. In all honesty, I often expect You to behave toward me the same way most men have.

I am not a man that I should lie. I do not change my mind. Have I ever spoken and failed to act? Have I ever promised and not carried it through?

Forgive me, God, but many times it seems You *have* failed to act. My brain knows You've always been with me, even throughout my childhood, but my heart has failed to experience Your presence. In August, You began to heal the wounds of my heart. Please continue to do so. And now, thank You for Your protection and provision during this storm. In Jesus' name.

"Are you all right?" Abby asked.

"Yeah, just having a conversation with God." I focused on God and allowed His presence to wash over me. I rested in His presence for a moment, then wiped the tears that had escaped as I prayed.

"God is so good. He told me He would protect and provide. Look for city lights," I told Abby. I scanned the road. I had no idea how big or little Ardmore was, but with the white-out conditions, I could probably drive right through town and never know it. Just like Abby prayed, the snowfall slowed and the wind let up. I spotted a building in the distance on the east side of the road.

"Thank you, God! Look, Abby."

"A church!"

Less than a quarter mile down the road stood a pristine white church complete with a steeple and bell. It would have blended in with snow-covered landscape except for the warm yellow-orange glow illuminating its windows. I spotted a dirt frontage road that led up to it.

"It's like a Thomas Kincaid painting." I drove the short distance to the frontage road, then turned. Another few yards and I pulled my Cruze to a stop at the side of the church. We both gazed out the windshield, astounded. Small but beautiful and inviting. The steeple stood tall, like a lighthouse beckoning all to safe harbors. Several deciduous trees bordered the north side of the building. No doubt they were a comforting source of shade in the heat of summer, but heir fall beauty had begun to fade. Now they stood like sentinels guarding the church, yet every gust of wind sent leaves raining down on the snow-covered ground. A tire swing hung from one tree, the wind whipping it wildly back and forth.

Abby and I looked at each other, wide grins across our faces.

I zipped my coat as far as it would go. Abby did the same. She hadn't come prepared for severe winter weather. Winter doesn't usually come to Missouri until late in November. This storm was a real fluke, but we weren't in Missouri anymore, Toto.

We hustled to the trunk as the wind and snow swirled around us, the storm beginning in earnest again. Abby grabbed my suitcase and hers. I pulled out the plastic tub with my winter emergency supplies, and we both rushed to the church door. Despite the warm glow of lights in the windows, I expected the doors to be locked, but a turn of the knob and a forceful push gave us entrance. I stepped inside with a sigh of relief. What better place for God to provide sanctuary from the storm than His own house?

"Sally, it's as beautiful inside as it is outside."

A fire crackled cheerily in an ancient wood-burning stove on the south side of the building. It warmed the large room to toasty comfort. A hexagonal light gray slate hearth surrounded the stove at least eighteen inches all around. The aged and well-worn hardwood flooring appeared to be walnut. Fifteen rows or so of old-fashioned carved wooden pews led up to the pulpit. A stained glass window depicting Christ's life, death, and resurrection shimmered behind the pulpit.

A shiver raced through my body as I walked up the center aisle. I had a sense of stepping back in time even though ceiling lights shone brightly.

"Hello?" I hollered.

"Hello."

Abby and I jerked around, startled by the voice. A thirty-ish, average-looking man walked toward the stove, his arms laden with wood.

"Are you all right?" he asked.

"Oh, uh…yeah…I was a bit surprised," I said. "I knew there must be someone here, but the place seemed so empty."

"I was outside." He dropped the wood next to the stove and brushed the dead grass and leaves from his coat sleeves. While he made his way over to us, he pulled off his gloves. "I'm Reverend Joshua Salem."

"Sally Clark, and this is my sister, Abby Reynolds." I smiled and clasped his hand. Warmth flooded through me like a hot spring at his touch. "Your church is an answer to prayer. Thought we were about to become a statistic of that blizzard." I released his hand and gazed into his sparkling brown eyes, searching for something that seemed familiar to me.

"I'm glad you weren't," he said as he shook Abby's hand. "I thought there would be a traveler or two who might need sanctuary. That's why I've got this stove going. Storms like this tend to wreak havoc with the electricity. I'm surprised it hasn't gone out before now." He turned and headed toward the back of the church. "Make yourselves comfortable. I've got to bring in more wood before the snow buries it. The weatherman says this may last for the next day and a half."

"I'll help. It's the least I can do since we're taking shelter here," I said.

"Thank you. I'll let you bring wood to this stove, and I'll stock the stove in my basement office."

"Works for me," I said cheerily, thrilled to be safe and warm.

"Where is here?" Abby asked.

"Christ Community Church. We're about five miles north of Ardmore and serve the rural community."

"Make yourself comfortable, Abby," I told her. "You're not dressed for this weather."

"I don't like that idea, but my fingers do tend to ache pretty quickly with the cold." Abby pulled off her jacket and tossed it onto a pew.

When Reverend Salem and I came to the back door, he stopped to put his gloves back on and rearrange the scarf around his neck. "Here," he said, grabbing a scarf from the hooks by the door. "Better put this on."

Knowing the bitter wind would slap me in the face again when I stepped outside, I wrapped it around my neck and over my mouth and nose.

We worked in silence for an hour or more. I brought the wood and Abby stacked it. Despite the cold, I worked up a bit of a sweat, and the wood pile steadily grew. I wondered how long the logs would last. More to the point, would the storm last as long as the weatherman predicted, and how cold would it get when night fell?

"That should do," Reverend Salem said as I stared at the stove. "Most certainly we're here for tonight and probably tomorrow night too. If the power goes out, I'll sleep up here so there won't be a need to keep the basement stove fully burning. That'll help our wood last longer."

"That's good to know. I'm not acquainted with wood burning stoves to know how quickly or slowly the wood disappears." I held my hands toward the stove to warm them. How could I feel sweaty and cold at the same time?

"I'm going back down to my office to work. You two make yourselves at home, and if you need anything, let me know." He smiled and left the room.

A fierce gust of wind slammed into the little church, making it creak and groan. The lights flickered, then regained their steady illumination. I made my way over to the window and watched the snow swirling in the fierce wind. What would the roads be like once the storm ended?

I turned my attention to the stained-glass window behind the pulpit now bathed in a flash of color. I wondered what Reverend Salem looked like while he delivered his message each Sunday with the sun casting its morning rays through the colored glass. Four large windows populated both the north and south walls. Two narrow windows framed the double front door on the west side of the church.

Now that I was safe and warm, my adrenaline dissipated and sleepiness overwhelmed me. "I'm suddenly very sleepy. Do you mind if I take a nap, Abby?"

"Not at all. Catch up on what you've missed lately. I might even join you."

I grabbed a blanket from my winter emergency kit and traipsed over to the pews closest to the stove. As I prepared to lie down, I noticed a thick red cushion. I didn't remember seeing cushions when I came in. Happy at the discovery, I curled up and drifted off to sleep.

Chapter Seven

"The fool has said in his heart, 'There is no God.'" Psalm 14:1a NKJV

Cohen Reed sped north on Hwy 71 at 80 mph. The thought of getting a speeding ticket on this deserted state highway didn't concern him even though the speed limit was sixty-five.

"Dad, don't you think you'd better slow down?" asked his twenty-year-old daughter, Hannah.

"You're right, but in all the times I've traveled this road, I've never seen a highway patrolman." He slowed the SUV to 65 despite his confidence he wouldn't be ticketed. "I'm a little concerned about this intermittent snow. It might get worse." He tried to relax. The survival of his business was riding on this conference. Hannah didn't know that, and he wasn't about to tell her. He had laid off his one employee six months ago. As much as he regretted the action, the business no longer had the income to pay the man's salary. Cash flow had improved a bit, but only temporarily. Snow or no snow, he had to get to Rapid City for the conference.

He turned on the radio and hit the seek button.

"...expecting blizzard conditions, so grab that milk and bread while you still can," the radio announcer said. "This is KNEB Better Country 94.1 FM in Scottsbluff. And now here's—"

"A blizzard in October? Terrific! Hannah, I don't care if I do get a ticket. We've got to get to Rapid City tonight. I can hardly deliver an opening keynote in the morning if I'm not there." Cohen floored the gas and the car jerked as the engine shifted gears in response.

Within thirty minutes the intermittent flurries escalated into heavy snow. Exasperated at having to drop his speed to fifty, the white-out conditions now forced him to drop to thirty.

Cohen huffed. At this rate, it could take till midnight to get to Rapid City, if he got there at all.

Out of the white abyss loomed a curve in the road, but much too late for him to react.

"Dad!" Hannah yelled.

He hit the brakes, knowing they'd still crash. Snow exploded in all directions as the car plowed into the ditch. The air bags erupted, the car jolted to a stop, and the engine died.

Cohen pushed the now-deflating air bag out of his face. He looked over at Hannah who was busy doing the same thing. "Hannah, are you all right?"

"Yeah, I think so. I hit my head somehow. I don't know, it's like the air bag pushed me into the window or something." She rubbed her forehead and looked over at Cohen.

"Let me see." He pulled Hannah's hand out of the way. "No bleeding; that's good. No bump, at least not yet, and there's no redness. Does it hurt?"

"Not really. I'm sure I'll be fine. But what do we do now? Are we going to be stuck in this blizzard in the car? We could freeze to death!"

"Calm down. Panicking isn't going to help the situation. We'll figure out something." He repositioned himself in the seat and rubbed his throbbing right wrist. The jolt of the crash had jerked his hand loose of the steering wheel. He wiggled his fingers but not without pain. He sighed and dropped his head onto the head rest.

He sat holding his painful wrist for several minutes, taking stock of the situation, and weighing the options. Several inches of snow covered the hood of the car, having flown across it with the impact.

Just last week he had discontinued his OnStar service. What lousy timing. He thought about calling 911. They could track his cell phone, determine where they were, and send help. But in this storm how many other people were doing the exact same thing? "I've got roadside assistance with the car insurance. I'll contact them. Can you shove the air bag out of the way enough to get into the glove box?"

Hannah messed with the air bag for a moment. "Nope. Now what?"

"I think I've got the info in my wallet." He reached around to his right back pocket. Pain shot up through his arm. He yelped and jerked his hand to his chest.

"Dad, what's wrong?"

"I hurt my wrist somehow." He cradled his wrist with his left hand. "Pull the insurance info out. The number for roadside assistance is on the back of the card."

Hannah dug through the various items in his wallet and found the card. Cohen pulled his cell phone out of the inside pocket of his suit coat and woke up the phone.

"I don't have any service. Do you?"

Hannah fished her phone from her purse. "No, I don't."

"Try dialing 911." He waited while Hannah replaced the insurance card then tapped out the number.

"That's strange. I'm not getting anything. Let me try your phone."

He handed her the phone and she dialed. She tilted her head and looked at him while they waited for the call to go through.

"Hmm." She held the phone out in front of her, looking at it with a deep frown across her lips. "Nothing but dead air."

She handed the phone back to him, and he thrust it back into his pocket. Could things get any worse?

Freezing to death in the car would probably qualify.

"Let's see if we can find a building nearby." He began to scan the area for a place they could take refuge in. With these conditions, they could be five yards from a gas station and not know it. After several minutes of staring into the white, he had spotted nothing.

"Dad, look! Almost right in front of us."

Cohen squinted to see through the onslaught of snow. He noticed a yellow-orange glow about fifteen or so yards from the car. Then he spotted a dilapidated dingy white church. The steeple stood tall, so he'd take a chance the rest of the roof was still in one piece. Several deciduous trees bordered the north side of the building. No doubt they were a comforting source of shade in the heat of summer, but their fall beauty had begun to fade. Now they stood like sentinels guarding the church, yet every gust of wind sent leaves raining down on the snow-covered ground. A tire swing hung from one tree and the wind whipped it wildly back and forth.

"Looks rather decrepit, but let's chance it. Grab your bag." He reached his right hand to the back seat to get his suitcase. Another shooting pain reminded him of his injured wrist, and he winced with pain.

"Are you going to be okay?" Concern covered Hannah's face.

"I'll be fine. It's probably just strained." He took a couple of deep breaths and waited for the pain to subside. Neither of them had thought to bring a winter coat. It was fall, after all. Not winter. He had a raincoat, Hannah her lightweight college jacket. They'd have to manage. "Okay, I'm ready. Wait for me beside your door."

He opened his door and climbed out. The moment he stood straight, the icy wind slapped him in the face. He shuffled his way to the back door and retrieved his suitcase. When he stepped out from the protection of the car, he lost his balance and fell as the wind slammed into him full force. He regained his bearings and headed over to Hannah.

"Let's link arms." Cohen waited while Hannah shifted her case to her right hand and then linked her left arm with his right. They bent into the wind to keep their balance, and as they took their first step, each sank several inches into the snow. Icy snow slid into his shoes. Now he'd have wet socks and cold feet. Why hadn't he checked the weather forecast? But who expects snow in October, especially when it was seventy degrees two days ago?

"Hannah, I'm going to fix my eyes on the church and start walking. I'm not taking my eyes off that building. I don't want to lose sight of it."

Hannah nodded her agreement.

"Take big steps. We'll support each other and take it slow if we have to. I think once we get out of the ditch the snow won't be so deep."

As they walked, the wind nearly ripped his suitcase from his hand, but he held tight. He'd need his clothes to stay warm if there was no heat in the church. They trudged on for several minutes, stopping at times to stay upright against the brutal wind, catch their breath, and ensure they were still headed in the right direction. The howl of the wind created an ambiance of a Stephen King horror movie. Terror was fine...as long as it was restricted to the TV screen.

He battled forward as his thoughts assailed him. *We have no food or water or any kind of survival kit. If the storm lasts into the night...if that church is empty and cold...if the temperature drops below zero...we'll be Popsicles by morning.*

Shivering, Cohen stumbled into the church, threw his suitcase to the floor, and fought the swirling wind in his struggle to shut the large wooden door. As he banged it closed, he leaned his back against it and stopped long enough to recover his breath from trudging through the blizzard. He assured himself of Hannah's safety. Her teeth chattered, and her nose, cheeks, and ears were deep red from the cold. He shot a look at the ceiling.

"I'm glad to see the roof is still intact, but the place is as dilapidated inside as it is outside." His hopes deflated as he examined the rest of the building. The place looked antiquated at best.

"I don't know, Hannah, we might have been better off staying in the car."

"You can't be serious!"

"Well, look at this place."

An ancient wood-burning stove occupied a portion of the south side of the church. A smattering of dead leaves covered the hexagonal slate hearth surrounding the stove. The stove could provide warmth, but he'd need wood to burn. Years of dust blanketed a good deal of the aged and well-worn hardwood floor. Several rows of pews on either side of a center aisle filled the room. Most of the pews on the left side of the aisle stood forlornly and charred. He could try to bust the charred pews and burn those. He went over to one pew and shook it, half-expecting it to fall apart. When it stood solid, Cohen sighed. *So much for that idea.*

The north wall, also charred, hosted four boarded windows. At the bottom of one sat a small pile of snow. And behind the pulpit the wall held nothing but peeling wallpaper. An eerie shiver raced through his body as he walked up the center aisle. Had he stepped back into the nineteenth century?

"I don't know, Dad, a few pews look burned, but other than that it looks solid. And it feels toasty warm."

"Right now anything would feel toasty after being out in that cold. At least all those windows are boarded over."

"What? I—" Hannah began.

"More refugees," said a voice that echoed from every corner of the room.

Cohen jerked his head around, looking for the source. He spotted a petite woman sporting a haircut shorter than his. She sat in a pew about halfway to the front and near the pot belly stove.

"Hello there," he said. He stomped the snow from his shoes and brushed it from the calves of his legs and his coat as best he could with one hand. Then he and Hannah made their way toward her.

"That storm is awful," Hannah said. "We crashed into the ditch."

"I didn't see the curve in the road," Cohen explained. "What a stroke of luck this place was less than fifteen yards away and that we even saw it."

"This church isn't luck; it's God's provision." The woman rose from the pew.

"Yeah, well, we might have been warmer if we'd stayed in the car." He scoffed.

"Good grief, no!" the woman said. "The heat is running and the wood stove has chased away the chill."

"Yeah, feels great in here to me." Hannah unbuttoned her coat.

Cohen raised an eyebrow at Hannah, then made his way over to the stove, his hand stretched toward it.

"Don't!" the woman yelled as he laid his hand on it.

On closer examination, the stove looked more ancient than the building. "This stove is stone cold, and it can't be much more than forty degrees in here. Haven't you seen that growing pile of snow over there?"

A look of astonishment flashed across the woman's face. She glanced toward the window he pointed at, her forehead crinkled in question. "I don't see any snow, and I can feel the heat of that stove from here." She stepped next to Cohen, shaking her head. "That stove is searing hot. I don't understand why your hand isn't burned."

He placed his hand on the stove again and then held it palm up for the woman to inspect. "See? No burns. It's ice cold."

The woman shook her head and stood staring dumbfoundedly at his hand.

"I'm Cohen Reed," he said, hoping to bring her out of her stupor.

"And I'm Hannah, his daughter."

"Sally Clark. Nice to meet you. My sister's here too, somewhere."

"I'm glad we found shelter," he said while he continued his examination of the church. "It's cold in here, but I guess it'll be warmer than being stranded in the car. By the looks of it, this place has been gutted by fire. At least those four broken windows are boarded over."

Sally looked confused, her head shaking yet again. Cohen watched her eyes flit from one wall to another and down to the pew she had been sitting in. "Fire? What are you talking about? It's a beautiful little country church. The pews are even cushioned. We'll have soft sleeping tonight."

Cohen walked around the room, looking at the charred walls and boarded windows on the north side of the building. And no cushions covered the pews. In addition to the mound of snow, a large pile of dead leaves populated a corner at the front of the church. Probably blew in before the windows got boarded.

"Things just got worse," he mumbled to himself. "Stuck in the middle of Nowhere, USA, in a church the wind could blow over any minute, and a crazy woman for company." He turned toward Sally. "Can't you see those places along the ceiling where the lath and plaster are exposed. The wallpaper is peeling everywhere, and that whole north wall is charred. Did you have a wreck too? Are you suffering from shock?"

"No."

"Then you're either half blind or suffering from hypothermia."

"Dad! There's no need to be rude."

"I'm neither," Sally said, "but no matter. I'm happy to have heat and that the electricity is still running."

"Electricity?" Hannah said. Cohen followed her gaze as she looked for evidence of electricity in the church. "How long have you been here?" she asked.

He watched Sally while she pulled her phone from her pants pocket and checked the time. "Only about an hour. I had just dozed off when you two came in. I haven't had lunch. I'm going to the kitchen for some food. Can I get you anything?"

"Coffee would be nice. But good luck with that," Cohen humored her. He pulled his coat collar up around his neck and looked at the ceiling again. No light fixtures. He wondered if the building ever had electricity or running water. The place reminded him of churches portrayed in the western movies he watched now and then. One room, hand-carved pews, a wood-burning stove to provide warmth, a front door, and maybe a back door leading to an outhouse.

He watched Sally disappear into the back of the church and then rested his hand on the stove again. It might be considered remotely warm if they were in the middle of Antarctica. Shoving his left hand under his armpit to stay warm, he groaned as full realization hit. This blizzard had buried any chances he had at saving his business.

Chapter Eight

"No wonder my heart is glad, and I rejoice. My
body rests in safety." Psalm 16:9 NLT

The church gutted by fire? Boarded windows? Peeling wallpaper? And the man calls me crazy? But his hand didn't get burned! How could that be? The stove is searing hot.

I pushed those thoughts aside and made my way to the basement to find Reverend Salem. I found him and Abby in his office, both on their knees. Knowing they must be in prayer, I hated to interrupt.

"Is there something I can do for you, Sally?" Reverend Salem asked as he turned to face me.

My eyebrows shot up, startled that he knew I was there.

"I heard your footsteps on the stairs," he said with a smile.

"Did you get any sleep?" Abby asked, getting up.

"Not really. Reverend Salem, I thought you should know, you have more company. A man by the name of Cohen Reed and his daughter, Hannah, arrived several minutes ago."

"I thought that might be the case. I heard the door bang and too many footsteps for one person. I'm glad this humble little church has saved others from the storm."

"I'm rather hungry. Would it be all right if I rummaged around the kitchen to see what there is to eat?" I asked.

"Certainly. All that I have is yours. If you two don't mind, I'll continue praying that others who need shelter find their way here."

I nodded in agreement, then took a brief look around his office. A 1940s-vintage walnut desk and chair occupied one corner of the small room. A wood-burning stove similar to the one upstairs stood next to the desk. Opposite the desk was a large armoire and matching bookshelf bulging with books. "Can I bring you anything? A sandwich, some coffee?"

"Thank you, but I'll get something after I've finished praying."

"Okay." I turned and Abby and I made our way upstairs to the kitchen. I marveled at the sense of peace I felt in the reverend's presence—like a quilt blanketing my soul with warmth and safety.

"God drew me downstairs to pray with Reverend Salem. His presence alone seems to warm the room. Did you notice?"

"Yes! I thought it was just me."

As we entered the roomy kitchen, I noticed an ancient General Electric refrigerator in the far corner. Next to it was a counter with a porcelain double sink. Cabinets lined two walls. A small walnut table flanked the third. The fourth wall was bare. Walnut must have been the wood of the day when the church was furnished.

"I don't see a coffee maker, but maybe we can boil some in a pot," Abby said.

I continued to peruse the room. "No stove either. How odd. No matter, we can cook on the wood stove out in the sanctuary. Best get the coffee brewing first, then make sandwiches. You start on that end of the cupboards, and I'll start on this end. Let's see what we can find."

As I searched the cupboards for a coffee pot, I found plenty of dry goods along with 1940s-style dishes. In the last cupboard I opened, I found a campfire coffee pot and next to it my favorite Folgers Breakfast Blend. A smile came unbidden as I pulled both from the cabinet. For some reason I had half-expected to find a blue metal can of Maxwell House circa 1945. Next to the coffee sat several cans of condensed soup. I grabbed a can of tomato.

"We've got coffee and soup." I filled the coffee pot with water and then spooned in the grounds. I imagined Cohen wrinkling his nose at it. Probably only Starbucks for him, but my tastes were simple. It appeared Reverend Salem's were too. "I'll see if there's milk in the fridge for this tomato soup. What have you found?"

"The pots and pans." Abby pulled out a pan and set it on the counter while I walked to the refrigerator. It stood quiet, but in faith I opened the door, fully expecting cold food. The GE didn't disappoint. I pulled out a loaf of bread and a package of pre-sliced cheese and laid them on the counter. Nothing said comfort like a grilled cheese sandwich and tomato soup. Next, I nabbed the carton of milk.

"Wow, Hershey's chocolate syrup in a can. Haven't seen that in ages," I said. Childhood memories of pouring Hershey's syrup over a bowl of ice cream popped into my head. A sense of having dropped back in time washed over me again. Odd how some items were as modern as the coffee, yet some, like the can of syrup and all the dishes, seemed straight out of a museum. Not quite *Twilight Zone* eerie, it left me feeling strange yet peaceful. As I popped the top on the soup, I began to hum "It Is Well with My Soul." I stopped mid-song.

"Abby, it *is* well with my soul, but not for my father's. I…I know I must forgive him…but it's so hard. Is he in hell or did he make it to heaven?"

"Only God knows that answer."

"Father went to church with me and Mom, but after Mom died that stopped." His behavior toward me never came close to Christian. But that didn't mean he hadn't had a conversion experience since I'd left home or maybe one after he went to prison. I stood quietly for a moment, listening for God's comforting voice.

I am not willing that any should perish, but that all should come to repentance.

The howl of the wind outside seemed to speak an audible response to God's heart.

Did that mean my father had perished?

"God, help me forgive him," I whispered. I turned back to the task at hand and finished prepping the soup while Abby made cheese sandwiches. We placed our goodies on some trays Abby had found and headed to the sanctuary.

Cohen, his suitcase open at his feet, had doffed his overcoat and suit coat and donned a sweater, then put his overcoat back on. No doubt to help him stay warm. For him the stove was ice cold. But Hannah had seemed to feel the warmth. Why? The pot belly stove did more than take the chill out of the air. The temperature in the room wouldn't rival Death Valley in summer, but it might manage to in winter.

"Coffee'll be hot in no time," I hollered.

"Oh my," Abby uttered. I peered at her. A spark of attraction lit her face as she stared at Cohen.

"You've got good taste. He's lean and handsome. And with those clothes, I bet he's a doctor or a lawyer," I whispered, "but I'd say he's at least ten years younger than you."

"So what? I can admire, can't I?" Abby said with a shrug of her shoulders. We set our trays on a pew and placed the coffee and pot of soup on the stove to heat.

"Don't get your hopes up," Cohen warned as he continued to rummage through his suitcase. "That stove couldn't fry a fly, let alone heat coffee."

"What does he mean the stove couldn't fry a fly?" Abby asked.

"He says the stove isn't hot. Know what's even weirder? He put his hand on it and didn't get burned."

"That *is* weird. I'll start the grilled cheese sandwiches as soon as the coffee's hot."

I returned to the kitchen to search for a hot pad and cups.

When I got back, Cohen and Hannah had joined Abby at the stove. I watched Cohen as he gazed first at the large skillet in Abby's hand and then at the cups and hot pad in mine.

"Do you really expect that coffee to cook on a cold stove?" he asked me.

"The stove feels hot to me, Dad," Hannah ventured.

"Only a fool would expect food to cook on a cold stove." I put my ear next to the pot and heard the coffee burbling. "And I'm neither a fool nor a crazy woman. That stove is plenty hot. All this will cook just fine."

I held out my hand with four cups ringed in my fingers. Cohen scoffed, not at all fazed by my rebuttal to his mumbled comment earlier about me being a crazy woman. He took a cup all the same. I reached for the coffee and began pouring.

When the steaming black brew spilled out to fill Cohen's cup, his mouth fell open. He dropped onto a pew, mouth still agape, and coffee sloshed out of his cup.

"Ouch!" He quickly set the cup down on the floor and shook the spilled coffee from his left hand, then rubbed at what had spilled onto his pants. He stared at the rising steam, then picked up the cup again and took a sip. "It's...hot!...I...how?"

He went to the stove and held the back of his right hand toward it. He looked at me, incredulous. He peered at the stove again and then down at the large pile of firewood next to it. "I never noticed that pile of wood before. I'm sure it wasn't there when I came in." He stared at Hannah as though for support for his observations.

"Don't look at me," she said. "I told you the stove felt hot to me."

"That stove burned hot when we arrived. Sally helped Reverend Salem stock the wood," Abby said while she got the sandwiches started.

"Who's Reverend Salem?" Hannah asked.

"The pastor of this church. He's in his office, praying," I explained.

"No one could possibly pastor this church. Look at it. That entire half of the building is burned out." Cohen waved his left arm toward the north side of the church. That's when I noticed the way he kept his right hand hugged to his chest.

"Mr. Reed, you seem to be favoring your right hand. Did you hurt it when you crashed?" I asked.

"Yeah, but I think it's just sprained."

"I don't know, Dad. You've yelped in pain several times."

Abby stepped over to him and gently held his arm out for inspection. "You need to keep this elevated and iced. I'll get some ice for you and then make you a sling."

"Are you a doctor?" Cohen and Hannah chimed.

"No, but you'd be surprised the things you learn growing up on a cattle ranch." Abby dashed off to the kitchen for ice. I didn't doubt she'd retrieve a pan full of snow if she couldn't find ice in the ancient GE.

Cohen sat down in the pew closest to the stove and took several more sips of his coffee. "This isn't half bad. Thanks."

"You're welcome," I said, a bit shocked. "I kinda figured you for a Starbucks guy."

"I prefer Caribou, actually." Cohen's eyes grew wide. "There are grounds sinking to the bottom of my cup." He sat watching his coffee, then turned, shook his head, and examined the stove again. "But I'm positive that stove...I mean, I put my hand on it. It was stone cold, and you saw my hand didn't have any burns."

Abby returned with a tea towel, some ice in a plastic bag, and a hand towel. Hannah helped him slip his arm out of his coat, then Abby created a sling out of the tea towel, wrapped the ice in the hand towel, and nestled it onto his wrist.

"There's a table and some chairs in the kitchen. As soon as you're done with your doctoring, Abby, why don't we grab them and bring them in here?" I suggested. "It's warmer here than in the kitchen, and we can sit closer to the stove than the pews afford. Plus, we'll have something to set our lunch on."

"Good idea," Hannah said.

Once done with Cohen, Abby examined Hannah. "Looks like you've got a bit of bump on your head. What did you hit it on?"

"The window. But I'm fine. It doesn't even hurt," Hannah insisted.

"Okay," Abby said skeptically. "A little ice on that wouldn't hurt either. I'll get you some."

"No, really, I'm fine."

I led the way into the kitchen and in quick order we three women had moved the table and five chairs to the sanctuary. By then the soup was done. I went back to the kitchen for bowls, and Abby started cooking the cheese sandwiches.

"Why five chairs?" Cohen asked Abby as I came back with the bowls.

"One for Reverend Salem. So, Mr. Reed, what has you out on the road in a storm like this?"

"Call me Cohen. I'm headed to Rapid City. I'm the keynote speaker for a business conference that starts tomorrow. Hannah came along for the ride." Cohen, who appeared to have finally gotten warm, shed his coat. His form-fitting beige sweater revealed a muscular frame, and his luxurious pants were a stunning glacier blue. Nothing cheap for this guy. He laid his overcoat across the arm of the pew and stood to warm himself at the stove.

"How about you? Where are you two headed?"

"Eventually, Montana," I said.

"Eventually?" Cohen said.

"We've been in Scottsbluff for family—"

"Scottsbluff! That's where we're from," Hannah said. "You must've left town shortly before we did. I'm surprised Dad didn't pass you on the road."

"I wasn't driving that fast." Cohen frowned at his daughter's comment. "You not only look alike, you sound exactly alike. I take it you're twins, or do you just have a tremendous resemblance as sisters?"

"We're twins," Abby said. "We were orphaned as babies and adopted by different families. We discovered each other this summer."

"How exciting!" Hannah squealed. "I can't imagine what a shock that must have been."

"You have no idea." Abby laughed. "I didn't even know I was adopted. My father's lawyer delivered that bit of news and that I had a twin sister in one fell swoop."

"Abby, you never told me that," I said.

"Guess I never thought about it." Abby flipped the sandwiches, the buttered bread sizzling when it hit the hot skillet.

"Abby lives in Montana. I live in Kansas City, but I'm going to visit after I'm finished with my business in Scottsbluff. I hope this blizzard isn't a taste of what's to come for the winter."

An awkward silence ensued, broken only by the whistle of the wind. Cohen poured a second cup of coffee and sat down in a pew. He pulled out his cell phone. "Blast, still no signal. That's western Nebraska for you."

"Actually, we're in South Dakota, but just," Abby said.

"I didn't have a signal earlier but maybe I do now." I pulled my phone out of the back pocket of my jeans and checked it. "Nope. Abby, do you?"

She retrieved her phone and checked it. "Do you need to make a call? I've got a signal now. Use mine." She held her phone out to him.

"Thanks. I need to let the conference coordinator know I'm stranded. It looks pretty unlikely I'll get to Rapid City today, despite how close we are." He offered a half smile, then turned his attention to the phone and walked to the back of the church.

"I wonder what he does for a living," I whispered to Abby.

"Whatever he does, he's obviously good at it. He's the keynoter."

"Dad's a business consultant," Hannah offered. "He helps businesses develop their branding and marketing."

"That's—" Abby said.

"Look, I'm sorry! You know what snow can do." Cohen's angry voice forced us to look toward him. He paced at the back of the church, still on the phone. The fire crackled as if in echo to the heat exploding from Cohen's conversation.

"Of course, I'll refund my fee if I don't get there. ...Yes, I understand. ...What?"

I tried not to listen, but it was impossible. He spoke loudly, angrily, and paced the floor less than twenty feet away.

"Even the airport is shut down and you're surprised I can't get there?" Cohen's tone struck me as sarcastic. "I'll do what I can to keep you posted." He disconnected the call and joined us at the table, handing Abby her phone. He sat down, releasing a deep breath as he did.

"Can you believe that? Not once did he ask if I was safe. Just worried about the advance fee he paid me."

"Did I hear you right? The airport is shut down?" Abby asked.

"Yeah. He said airport officials shut things down about thirty minutes ago. It's snowing so hard they can't keep the runways clear, besides which there's zero visibility." Cohen stood and walked to the window. "Same thing here."

A gust of wind howled like a coyote baying at the moon. The building shuddered. The lights flashed and went dark.

"I guess it was only a matter of time before the electricity went out," I said.

"What are you talking about? How do you know the electricity went out?" Cohen asked.

"Because the lights went out." I looked up and pointed to the ceiling lights. I watched as Cohen and Hannah examined the ceiling.

"There are no light fixtures," he insisted. He looked at Hannah who shrugged her shoulders. "I don't suppose you noticed any flashlights in the kitchen?"

"No, but I've got one in my winter emergency kit, and I saw some hurricane lamps in Reverend Salem's office." I jogged over to the plastic tub I used for winter emergency supplies and pulled out the flashlight. "We don't need it now, but it'll be handy when we do."

"Tell me about this conspicuously absent reverend," Cohen said sarcastically.

"Whether you believe me and Abby or not doesn't change the fact that he's here. I'm sure he'll come upstairs later when it gets dark outside. For now, let's eat."

I poured soup for those of us who wanted it, and Abby scooped sandwiches straight from the skillet to plates. We ate in silence, though I watched Cohen and Hannah telegraph each other through eye contact.

"How about we play some cards to pass the time once we're done cleaning up from lunch? I've got a deck in my winter emergency kit."

"That's certainly better than just sitting here," Abby said.

"I'm down for that. Dad, can you manage?" Hannah asked, looking at him over by the window.

"It won't be easy with one hand, but I might as well," Cohen said. He slowly turned from the window and took a seat at the table again. Something about him reminded me a lot of my father.

First remove the log from your own eye. Cohen is none of your business. Forgive your father.

Ouch! Years ago, I had learned to recognize my heavenly Father's voice and to never ignore it. Discipline was never pleasant, godly or otherwise. I knew I had to forgive my father, but despite my forty years of absence, ten years of his alcoholic outrages and abuse during my childhood still haunted me.

Hannah helped Abby clear the table and take all the dishes to the kitchen. The three of us washed and dried the dishes, then I dug out the deck of cards, and we all sat down at the table to play.

"Does everybody know how to play 500 rummy?" I shuffled the cards. They nodded and so I began to deal the cards.

I'd deal forgiveness later.

Playing cards had eased the tension, so I ventured some small talk.

"So, Cohen, have you always lived in Scottsbluff?"

"No. I grew up in Chadron."

"If you don't mind me asking," Hannah said, "how did you two learn about each other?"

"I received an inheritance back in August from Abby's father."

"How did you know Abby's father and not Abby?" Cohen asked. His question surprised me. He had projected nothing but sullen silence all during our card game.

"I didn't know her father, not really."

"So why did he leave you an inheritance if you didn't know him?" Hannah questioned.

"I sort of knew him. I met him and his wife while they were vacationing in Paris."

"Paris! Such a romantic city." Hannah sighed. "I'd love to visit there someday."

"I didn't take you for a world traveler. Must have been a nice vacation for you," Cohen said.

"Oh, she wasn't there on vacation," Abby chimed in. "She was based there with the Marine Corps."

"Well, that certainly explains your die-hard attitude," Cohen said.

"Don't be insulting," Abby reprimanded him.

"I'm not. Sally probably considers that a compliment. Marines are tough, taught to survive." Cohen stared at me as if he expected me to offer my agreement.

"Yes, we're tough, but I think it was your tone Abby objected to," I said. As Abby and I stared at Cohen, he turned a bit red.

"Then I apologize for my tone." He looked at Abby as he spoke.

I couldn't discern the emotion that veiled his face. I sat a bit stunned that he sincerely apologized. "Apology accepted."

We continued with another hand of 500 as the wind moaned and the snow piled higher. At one point, Abby got up and added some wood to the stove, and Cohen traipsed to the south window for the umpteenth time.

"Do you think by looking out the window you can stop the snow?" I asked.

"I wish," he grumbled. "I just want to keep an eye on it. If there's any chance of getting to Rapid City yet today, I've got to take it."

"But, Dad, how can we get anywhere with our car crashed into the ditch?"

Cohen collapsed into his chair. "How could I forget that? Da— "

I assumed he was about to curse and caught himself.

"Was there much damage to your car?" Abby asked.

"I don't know. The airbags blew. The front end is buried in snow in the ditch. Blast!" He bolted up from his chair, knocking it over in his haste.

"Look, you might as well resign yourself to being here for a day or two. The radio said the forecast was for this storm to last thirty-six hours." I watched as he righted his chair and made his way to floor-to-ceiling windows that flanked the front door.

"I can't even see the car! No way are any of us getting to Rapid City today or tomorrow." Cohen groaned.

Abby rose from her seat and made her way over to him. "Think of it this way, if you can't make it there, neither can the conference attendees. Maybe it'll get postponed or canceled. You and your daughter are here, safe and warm, and not stranded in the car on the highway."

Leave it to Abby to find a way to encourage someone. She found the positive in everything. Did I? Or did I automatically expect the negative?

"Abby's right, Dad. I'm so glad we're here and not freezing to death—literally—in the car." Hannah approached her father and hugged him.

"I guess you're right. I guess you're both right. I need to let it go, but I was really hoping I'd get some new business clients at this conference."

By now, we were all standing at the front door, staring out the windows. We might as well have been staring at a white sheet. I hadn't seen snow like this since I was a kid. We might be stuck here for several days, but I kept my suspicions to myself.

Chapter Nine

"Unless I see in His hands the print of the nails, and put
my finger into the print of the nails, and put my hand
into His side, I will not believe." John 20:25b NKJV

Excuse me, ladies, I need the restroom," Cohen announced
when they finished the last hand of 500 rummy. "As ancient as
this place is, there's probably only an outhouse."

"I'll grant you, this place is old, but not ancient." Sally pushed back
her chair. "There's only one bathroom in the basement, but it's quite
nice. Follow me."

They rose from the table. Sally grabbed her flashlight and led him
down a dark hallway.

"Just down these stairs, first door on your right. Here, you'll probably need this." She handed him the flashlight, and with a smile headed
back toward the sanctuary. His irritation level rose. Why did she get
under his skin? Nothing seemed to bother her, and she had an answer
for everything. In fact, she seemed quite at home in this burned-out
old church. Abby and Sally might look alike, but they had very different personalities. He smiled as he thought about Abby and how ten-
derly she had handled his wrist.

He shoved that thought away and before heading down the stairs,
panned the flashlight around to get a look at things. He hadn't ventured out of the sanctuary even to help bring in the table and chairs.
Both the women and Hannah had insisted he sit and rest his wrist. Off

to his left from where he stood at the top of the stairway, he spotted the church kitchen. He poked his head in for a look-see.

Despite the coming dusk, the day still provided enough light for him to see without using the flashlight. One lone chair stood against a wall, giving the room a forlorn, abandoned feel. Cobwebs populated every corner of the ceiling.

He turned to the stairway, aimed the flashlight toward the basement, and carefully made his way down the narrow steps. He shivered from the cold assaulting him as he descended the stairs into the nearly pitch black hallway. Must not be any windows in the basement.

He spotted the first doorway. The door was open. He took one step in. What little light the flashlight afforded him revealed peeling wallpaper, a rust-stained toilet and sink, and nothing with which to wipe his hands dry. He supposed for a Marine this probably was *quite nice.* He tended to business and quickly returned to the warmth of the sanctuary. Abby and Sally were sitting at the table. Hannah was over by the pulpit, staring at a blank wall.

"Hannah, what in the world are you looking at?" he asked.

She glanced at him and then back at the wall. "This beautiful stained-glass window. It depicts the life, death, and resurrection of Jesus. I…I don't know how I missed seeing it when we first came into the church."

Cohen squeezed his eyes shut and then looked again. He saw a blank wall with peeling wallpaper. The same thing he'd noticed when they got there. No stained-glass window. But he wasn't up for an argument. He let it drop and turned to Abby.

"Abby, where did you find that food you and Sally made for lunch?" He took a seat.

"In the kitchen, of course."

"But I was just in there. I didn't look in the cupboards—too many cobwebs—but that museum-piece of a refrigerator couldn't possibly still be working." He watched as Abby looked over at Sally. Both had furrowed eyebrows.

"Cohen, there are no cobwebs," Abby said. "The refrigerator is working just fine and is full of food. So are the cupboards. You made a comment earlier about the stove not being able to 'fry a fly.' I'm a little concerned. Did you hit your head and not realize it?"

"No. How could I hit my head and not know it? Do you see a bump anywhere?" He threw his arms in the air in exasperation but was immediately sorry he had. He sighed. "The airbag smacked me in the face, but I'm pretty sure I didn't hit my head on the steering wheel."

"Maybe it's just your pain affecting your perception of things," Sally offered.

"If I was delirious with pain, I wouldn't be sitting here talking to you."

"Good point." Sally shrugged and looked at Abby.

"I can't explain it. But let me take a look at your wrist and see if the swelling has gone down." Abby rose from her chair and walked to his side of the table. He held out his arm as far as the sling would permit and allowed Abby to do whatever she needed. Just this bit of movement brought on pain and he winced.

"Sorry," Abby said.

"Can't be helped." He looked up at her. She was focused on her work, but he noticed the compassion in her sky blue eyes. Now that he was thinking more clearly than when he first entered the church, he observed several other things. The gentleness of Abby's touch, the hint of a smile ever-present on her lips, and the faint scent of carnations. His attraction to her surprised him.

"The swelling hasn't gone down, but it isn't any worse either. That's good."

Abby looked at him and for a moment, their eyes met. "Thank you, Abby. It feels much better than when I got here. I appreciate your skills." Cohen watched Abby blush at his words.

"You're more than welcome." Abby glanced at Sally, then moved back to her seat. "I wonder if Reverend Salem fell asleep. I'm surprised he hasn't been up here before now."

"Reverend Salem? Oh yeah, the non-existent preacher," Cohen said.

"Non-existent nothing. Do you think I dragged in all that firewood by myself?" Sally pointed to the wood piled beside the stove.

"Well...yeah, I did." Cohen examined the darkened walls and the charred pews on the north side of the room. "Half the building is a charred mess. There's no way any preacher still preaches here." He watched as Sally and Abby looked around the room, their expressions puzzled again.

"Charred mess? Like I said before, this is a beautiful church, right down to the stained-glass window behind the altar." Sally turned and pointed at the window. Cohen followed her line of sight, snickered briefly, then caught himself. Hannah still stood there admiring that self-same window.

He wondered whether this deranged female Marine might not, at any moment, become a *violent*, deranged female Marine.

"There is no stained-glass window. It's a blank wall with peeling wallpaper and loose plaster. A pile of leaves stands where the pulpit should be. You're delusional."

"Then I am, too," Abby blurted.

"And me." Hannah returned to her seat at the table.

"That's three out of four. Majority rules. You're the one who's delusional," Sally accused.

"Sally, stop. You sound like a bratty teenager," Abby said.

Cohen smirked, thinking he'd won that argument.

"Listen, Cohen. Sally and I prayed for God to provide a safe place for us to ride out the storm. Five minutes later, we pulled up to the front door of this church. It's old, I'll give you that, but the walls are clean and white, and hymnals are neatly placed on the pews. Besides, we met Reverend Salem shortly after we got here. He's in his office."

"Show me," Cohen demanded. "I was just in that basement, and it was *very* cold and *very* dark."

"I don't think we should disturb him. He's praying," Sally said.

"A convenient excuse. I'll believe you when I see him." Cohen frowned. Considering our situation, you sure seem calm and confident."

"I am." Sally shrugged. "I trust God to watch out for me and Abby. And He is. You thought the stove was cold, and how did that turn out?"

"Whatever." Cohen rolled his eyes. "You're a religious nut on top of being a lunatic." He hadn't meant to say those words. They simply tumbled out along with his frustration at her peaceful demeanor.

"That's uncalled for." Abby gave him a withering stare. "Just because you've turned your back on God because your business is failing is no reason to insult my sister and me."

Cohen jumped out of his chair. He stood staring at Abby in the heavy silence of the room as if the weight of the snow on the roof would cave in on them at any moment.

"I...you...how...my business isn't—" Cohen attempted. As he worked to lie about his business, he noticed a man standing in the hallway entrance, holding two glowing hurricane lamps. Something deep inside Cohen compelled him to speak the truth. He looked Abby in the eye. "How do you know my business is failing?"

"I imagine because God told her," a man said.

Cohen jerked his head toward the guy, now realizing he wasn't a figment of his imagination.

"I'm Reverend Joshua Salem. Sorry not to have greeted you sooner, but I've been praying and preparing a sermon. I didn't want to lose my train of thought. You weren't in a hurry to leave, were you, Cohen?"

"Actually, yes." Cohen met the reverend's extended right hand with his left. Heat coursed through him like a hot poker at the man's touch. He was average looking, about thirty. But as Cohen peered into Reverend Salem's piercing brown eyes, he expected to see a fire that matched the inferno emanating from his hand.

"It's been awhile since you've been in a church, hasn't it, Cohen?"

"How would you know that?" Cohen pulled his hand free from the reverend's grasp.

"I can see it in your eyes."

"Yes, well...How did you know my name?"

"My heavenly Father told me, but so did Sally."

Cohen tried not to roll his eyes. Now he had three nut jobs to deal with. "I seem to recall a story from the Bible that said Jesus calmed the storm. Why don't you ask Him to do that now?"

"The Bible also says 'For He says to the snow, "Fall on the earth."'"

"I needed to get to Rapid City, and this storm really messed things up," Cohen grumbled. "My car's wrecked and I hurt my wrist."

"I'm glad you found a safe haven here rather than being stranded in your car." The reverend set the hurricane lamps on the table.

"Cohen," Sally said, "even if your car wasn't wrecked and the storm stopped this very moment, you wouldn't be able to get to Rapid City."

"Yeah? Why's that?" Cohen tried to tame his rudeness.

"Because the roads are probably a mess. It takes time to clear them," Sally answered.

A gust of wind made the church shudder, and everyone stood with their ears tuned to the storm outside.

"We're perfectly safe here. The building is sound," Reverend Salem assured them.

"That's a matter of opinion." Cohen stomped toward the window.

The raging winter storm mirrored the tension in his gut. He thought about the presentation he was to give at tomorrow's conference and that he was not going to get there. He thought about his failing business, that he couldn't refund the advance speaking fee because he'd already spent it to pay his mortgage. But mostly he thought about what Abby said and how she knew his business was failing. More than that, had she hit on the truth when she said he had turned his back on God? This place was having an odd effect on him, and he wasn't sure he liked it.

The double front doors flew open, startling everyone. As the doors banged into the walls and bounced back, frigid air whooshed in, carrying plenty of snow with it.

Everyone hurried over. Cohen and Reverend Salem each grabbed a door and fought to shut it.

Reverend Salem examined the doors. "The latch is broken." His brown hair blew wildly in the wind that whistled its way through the slight opening between the doors.

"And you said the building was sound." Cohen cradled his wrist with his left hand. "Now what do we do? We can't stand here all night holding the doors shut. My wrist is pounding."

"Let's stack some pews up against them," Reverend Salem said. "Abby, Hannah, can you hold the doors shut while Sally and I carry over a pew or two."

"They're not bolted down?" Sally asked.

"Thankfully for this situation, no," Reverend Salem explained. "Do you think you can handle the weight? Cohen's out for the count."

"I keep in shape. I'm sure I'll manage."

Abby shouldered her way into Reverend Salem's position on the door, and Hannah took Cohen's place. They managed to keep the doors tightly shut and the snow and cold air out as Sally and Reverend Salem jogged to a pew and lifted it. Cohen walked to a seat near the stove and sank down to watch the production.

"Holy cow, this is heavier than I expected." Sally straightened her knees as they lifted the pew.

"How are you going to put that against the doors with me and Abby standing here?" Hannah asked.

"We'll get as close to you as we can and still give you wiggle room to slide out the sides." Reverend Salem and Sally lurched toward the doors. "That should minimize how far the doors open. We'll all have to move fast. Let's set this down for a moment."

Cohen watched as they set down the pew. Sally took in a deep breath, obviously feeling the exertion of lifting it. He looked at it and wondered how such flimsy wood could be so heavy.

"Sally and I will ease this next to you two, and on the count of three, you each move as quickly as you can to opposite ends, and then we'll push it up against the doors."

"Works for me," Abby said.

"And me," Hannah said.

Cohen stood by watching it all, helpless to do anything with his injured wrist.

"Everybody ready?" Reverend Salem and Sally bent down and got a new grip on the pew. "One…two…three."

As Hannah and Abby scrambled sideways as quickly as they could, the doors burst open again, slamming into the back of the pew. As soon as Abby and Hannah were clear, Reverend Salem and Sally pushed against the flapping doors and dropped the pew into place.

They all stood watching and waiting to see if one pew would hold.

The pew stayed in place, but not flat against the doors due to the elaborate casing around the doorway.

"Is there something we can wedge in here to make up the difference?" Sally jumped up on the pew and pushed the doors shut to keep out the cold.

"Maybe there's a piece of wood in the pile that will work." Reverend Salem hurried to the stove and began digging through the pile. He held up a chunk. "This might work." He jogged back, knelt next to Sally, and shoved the chunk of wood between the doors and the back of the pew.

Sally released her hold. Cohen held his breath, waiting to see if the wood would hold.

"Hallelujah! Looks like it's going to work." Sally stepped down off the pew. The moment she did, the chunk of wood fell to the floor.

"How about turning the pew perpendicular to the door. Maybe one pew for each door?" Cohen suggested.

"Good idea. I'll take this end, Sally, you grab the other." Reverend Salem stepped to one end. "I'll push; you pull."

Cohen watched as the two inched the pew across the doors until Sally's end sat close to where the two doors met. "OK, Rev, slide your end out. Abby, while he does that, can you jump in there and be ready to hold the door shut if needed while they maneuver the pew against the doors?"

"Yeah, I can manage that." Abby took her position and nodded her readiness.

"On three, Reverend," Cohen said. "One, two, three!"

In a flurry of movement, they swung the pew perpendicular and swiftly pushed it against the door.

"Let's use two pews." Reverend Salem and Sally lifted another and placed it next to the first one. They spent a minute repositioning them until they were certain they would hold.

"Teamwork!" the reverend said. "Let's grab these cushions, and we can use them tonight as extra padding to sleep on. In fact, we can all grab cushions from the pews to give us extra comfort for the night."

"What cushions are you talking about, Rev?" Cohen asked.

Reverend Salem looked at Cohen and then at Sally and Abby. He gave them a wink. Were cushions an inside joke?

"This one, Cohen." He leaned over, grabbed the cushion from the pew, and handed it to Cohen who stood there dumbfounded.

There had been no cushions on the pews. He walked up the center aisle, examining each row. "There are no cushions here!"

"Look again." The reverend nodded his head toward Cohen, encouraging him.

He shut his eyes for a moment, then opened them again. Every one of the pews now held three-inch thick red cushions. "I…I." He shook his head. "I swear these weren't here."

"You obviously aren't very observant." Sally grabbed a cushion, shook it at Cohen, then laid it back on the pew. "I don't know about anyone else, but I'm hungry. That cheese sandwich and soup at 2:30 didn't stick with me very long,"

"Why don't you three resourceful ladies see what you can rustle up for supper. I'd like to talk with Cohen for a minute," Reverend Salem said.

Cohen watched Abby, Sally, and Hannah walk to the kitchen, then turned back to Reverend Salem. "What did you need to talk to me about?"

"About your negative attitude. Don't you realize how what you say affects those around you, especially Hannah?"

Cohen closed his eyes, took a deep breath, and slowly let it out. "Gonna play the guilt card, huh, Reverend?"

"If that's what it takes to get through your frostbitten soul."

"That's harsh. Isn't God all about love?"

"Yes, and He loves you despite the fact that you've turned your back on Him. Even when you were going to church, you were spiritually dead," Reverend Salem said.

Cohen approached the reverend, ready to get up in his face if needed. He leaned forward, his left hand raised and finger pointed, but his aggressive posture didn't appear to intimidate the reverend. "Where do you get off saying that, and how would you know?"

"I know the same way Abby knew you blame God for your business's failure. Because my Father told me."

Cohen collapsed into a pew as if the gale outside had blown him over. *How do they know my business is failing? I must be dreaming. Maybe I crashed harder than I thought and I'm...dead and caught in a living nightmare.* Cohen shook his head, willing his wild thoughts into oblivion.

"Cohen!" Reverend Salem hollered.

He shook his head again and brought his attention back to the reverend. "What did you say?"

"I said, you are not caught in a living nightmare."

This guy is a mind reader. How does he know these things? Cohen stood and Reverend Salem continued.

"You're like Thomas of the Bible. When the disciples told him Jesus was alive, Thomas said, 'Except I shall see in his hands the print of the nails, and put my finger into the print of the nails, and thrust my hand into his side, I will not believe.' Sally and Abby believe God will take care of them because they know the Bible says He will. They see the needed provision because they first believed and had faith for it. But you? You don't believe and don't see until it's proven to you."

This has got to be a dream, but it's the most bizarre dream I've ever had. Cohen pinched his arm as if to wake himself up.

"You are not dreaming, Cohen. Believe God. Let 'the LORD is my shepherd' be a reality in your life."

"Stuff it, Reverend" Defiance rushed through Cohen's veins like an Old Faithful eruption as he stood staring at the man.

"'Death and life are in the power of the tongue: and they that love it shall eat the fruit thereof.' You can speak life and provision for this situation or you can speak death and lack. The choice is yours. Just realize it impacts Hannah."

"Enough! I don't *want* your sermons and I don't *need* your sermons. Now leave me alone." Cohen stalked off to the window he'd periodically stared out of all afternoon. He couldn't see anything but his own reflection. Wrinkles creased his brow and haggardness etched his face. He sighed and turned to face the other way.

Chapter Ten

"The land you have given me is a pleasant land." Psalm 16:6a NLT

As I led Abby and Hannah to the kitchen to prepare dinner, I began praying in the Spirit. I sensed that more than Cohen's business and the storm weighed on his mind like a ticking time bomb he believed might explode at any moment.

"Why don't you two see what you can find in the cupboards." I set a hurricane lamp on the counter. "I'll search through the refrigerator. We can prep everything in here."

As we each went about our tasks, I continued to pray under my breath while I quickly searched the fridge. "Wow, look at this! There's a package of bratwurst in the icebox. That'll cook easily and quick enough. I wonder if there's any *brötchen*."

"Brorchen? What's that?" Abby asked.

"Brötchen," I pronounced it again. "It's German for *little bread*, a bun. I spent time in Germany when I was in the Corps. The first time I ever ate bratwurst was in Frankfurt." I pulled the bratwurst from the ancient icebox and set it on the counter. "I always say brötchen because that's the first word that comes to mind when I think bratwurst. And they served it with this delicious mustard! Not at all like our yellow mustard. Bratwurst and *pommes frittes*...french fries." I smacked my lips as I remembered my favorite food from my short stint in Germany.

"Here's a can of beans." Hannah held up the can she'd found. "I hope we can find a can opener."

"The can opener is in that drawer." Joshua entered the kitchen. "How's it going, ladies?"

"Great. I hope you like bratwurst and beans," I said.

"I do." He began rummaging through the cupboards.

"What're you looking for?" Abby asked while scouring the drawer for the can opener.

"I think there might be some brötchen here somewhere. One of my congregants is a German lady who makes them for me all the time. Only way to eat bratwurst. There might even be some German mustard in the fridge."

"Reverend Salem, I could kiss you!" I held out my hands and looked at him.

He pulled his head back and raised his eyebrows at me. "I trust you mean that rhetorically?"

"Of course. I miss authentic German bratwurst and brötchen. What I can get here in the US doesn't compare."

Hannah and Abby stood, mouths agape, but with a hint of a smile.

"I came to wash my hands. Seems I cut myself moving that pew." Joshua pulled a bag of brötchen from the top shelf of the cupboard, then moved to the sink. I watched as he turned on the hot water with his right hand and held his left under the water. The palm of his hand was covered in blood.

"Reverend, that doesn't look good." I moved to his side. "Are there bandages anywhere?"

"Not that I recall. It'll be fine. I'll just wrap my handkerchief around it." He shut off the water, pulled his kerchief from his back pocket, and wrapped his hand. "Good as new," he said and left the room.

"How did he know you wanted those buns?" Abby asked after he left.

"Probably heard me say it just like he heard Hannah say she needed a can opener."

We fell silent, each preparing things for dinner. I went back to my prayer, my lips moving in silence. The Bible says God is Jehovah-Jireh, God who provides, and He was certainly fulfilling that promise.

"Thank you, Father," I said under my breath and continued to pray for provision and protection during the storm.

I put the bratwurst and some water in the cast iron skillet we had used to grill our cheese sandwiches. Hannah found a pot and dumped in the can of beans, and Abby collected plates and glasses from the cupboard.

"Sally, can I ask you a personal question?" Hannah asked.

"Sure. Fire away."

"Do you always talk to yourself when you're fixing dinner?" Hannah gave a nervous chuckle.

I gave her a reassuring smile. "I'm not talking to myself. I'm praying in tongues. I can't pray that way without actually saying it."

"I know what you mean," Abby said. "It comes from our spirit, not our head. That's why. Are you a believer, Hannah?"

"Yes, and I've gone to church since I was a little girl, but I always heard praying like that was from the devil."

"When the 120 in the upper room were filled with the Spirit, they all started speaking in tongues. Would God give them something that was from the devil?" Abby said.

Hannah looked at Abby then at me, her forehead wrinkled in question. "Good point."

"Praying in tongues is praying in your own special language that goes straight to God. The apostle Paul said in Corinthians somewhere 'I thank God that I speak in tongues more than any of you.' It's not from the devil. Don't be afraid to embrace it," I told Hannah.

"I'll give it some thought. But you know, I don't understand my dad. I mostly see what you two see about this church. How come he doesn't?"

"Probably because he has an unbelieving, unwilling heart," Abby said.

"That seems harsh. My dad is a good man."

"I didn't mean to say he wasn't." Abby reached out to Hannah. "But if he doesn't believe in God, then he can't see what the kingdom of God provides."

I leaned back in my chair, my stomach stuffed from dinner.

"Thank you for dinner, ladies. I haven't had bratwurst in ages." Joshua wiped his mouth and placed his paper napkin on his plate. "I'm going to retreat to my office and continue my prayers. Please excuse me."

"What do you expect that to accomplish, Reverend?" Cohen asked.

"Prayer brought you here, didn't it?" Joshua stood from the table. He shrugged and peered back at Cohen.

"I needed to get to Rapid City, not be stuck here in the middle of nowhere!"

I looked across at Abby. She didn't appear uncomfortable at Cohen's outburst like I was. His behavior was too reminiscent of my father for my comfort.

"God is watching over us," Joshua said. "'We know that all things work together for good to them that love God, to them who are the called according to his purpose.' And you are called, Cohen. You've gotten lost along the way, but you are called."

"Put a sock in it!" Cohen grumbled and stood from the table. "Go pray. I'll be glad to be free of your holier-than-thou attitude."

Cohen had been mostly pleasant all afternoon. What had turned him so mean? His anger didn't faze Joshua who merely smiled and headed for his office. I heard a whoosh of breath from Cohen as Joshua stepped out of sight.

"We could be stuck here for days," Cohen said to the room. "Who knows how long that storm will rage or how long it will take highway maintenance crews to clear the roads once the snow does stop. And no amount of prayer is going to keep that wood pile from running out. I doubt the food will last that long either."

"Are you forgetting you insisted the wood-burning stove was ice cold. Remember how that turned out?" I said from my place at the table. "God didn't provide us shelter, warmth, and food today just to let us freeze to death a few days from now."

"And you can put a sock in it too!" Cohen pointed his finger at me.

"Grouch all you like, but our words hold the power of death and life. If you want to freeze and go hungry, that's your business." I stood and my voice rose in anger. "Personally, I'm cozy warm and well fed, and I trust God to keep me that way for the duration. I don't need or want your words impacting me in negative ways!"

"I'll say what I want to say!" Cohen yelled.

"Oh, I see, you can say whatever you want, but the reverend and I have to put a sock in it."

"Dad, stop!" Hannah hollered. "Arguing is only going to make matters worse."

"I'm sorry." I took my seat again. I looked over at Abby, surprised she kept silent. "I didn't mean to lose my temper. I guess we're all keyed up more than we realize." I drew a deep breath to calm myself. The storm didn't have me worried, but Cohen's behavior reminded me too much of my father, and I half expected him to slap me across the face. Like Abby had said earlier, I seemed to be reverting to teenage behavior. My father's abusive words resounded in my head. How was that possible after being away for forty years? God, heal those wounds. Help me forgive my father. I can't do it without Your help.

Hannah's words seemed to bring Cohen to his senses as well. I watched as he sat down next to her.

"Hannah, I'm sorry. I...I really needed to get to that conference. It was my last chance to turn my business around."

"How can a conference turn your business around?" Abby asked.

"I'd garner new clients. My business has been failing for more than six months. The cash flow has all but dried up. I had to let go of my one employee because I couldn't afford to pay him anymore." Cohen responded so patiently and kindly to Abby, yet he acted the opposite toward me.

"You don't owe me an explanation," Abby said.

"But I'd like to explain. And Hannah deserves to know." Cohen stood and retreated to a pew. Hannah and Abby followed him, each sitting on either side of him.

Why did he want to explain things to Abby who was a total stranger?

"It's my job to provide for my family. Hannah wants to participate in an exchange program in Switzerland. Until now, she hasn't known that money is tight—"

"But, Dad, all you had to do was tell me. I'm not unreasonable."

"I don't want you to you see me as a failure."

I watched as Abby covered Cohen's left hand with hers. "The business may fail, but that doesn't make you a failure. Surely your wife has told you that. Or does she not know either?"

"My wife divorced me some years ago."

"I'm sorry. I didn't mean to bring up painful memories."

Cohen looked at Abby, but I couldn't discern his emotion.

"If things don't turn around, I may be facing bankruptcy."

"Oh, Dad!"

"Maybe God is using this situation to get your attention." Abby said. "He's provided for us here. He'll continue to. He can show you what to do about the business, but you have to ask Him and believe."

This guy was hard to figure out. I'd known few men in my life who hadn't treated me like an object designed for their pleasure. Yet, here was Cohen pouring his heart out to a perfect stranger, admitting things about himself that most men never would. Certainly nothing my father ever did. I often wondered why my mom married him.

Maybe he never allowed you to see his soft side. He adopted you, didn't he?

He gave in to my mom's desire for a child, God. And You know full well how many times he said I was not his daughter.

What was I thinking, arguing with God? Not good. I turned my attention back to Abby and Cohen.

Abby kept her hand over Cohen's and deepened her gaze at him. I caught the attraction between the two of them, but did they notice it themselves? Cohen's behavior had been like good-cop, bad-cop. Another reminder of my father…and Jake Bonner, the man who had tried to kill me.

Bitterness is the fruit of unforgiveness. And, Sally, bitterness grips your heart. It has tainted all your relationships with men, and especially your relationship with Chase. You must root out both the unforgiveness and the bitterness.

I sat and considered what the Holy Spirit said. I didn't doubt His words. I had struggled with forgiving my adoptive father since I'd left home to join the Corps. Heavenly Father, You know how much I've battled with this. I need Your help to do it.

You only need to ask.

Okay, Father, tonight, after everyone goes to bed.

I once again turned to watch Abby, Cohen, and Hannah. My attention had been diverted long enough that Abby had disappeared. I searched the sanctuary for her but didn't see her anywhere.

"It'll be all right, Dad. I don't have to go to Switzerland. I don't have to go to college. I can get a job for a while. Maybe then I'd be more certain about what I really want to do with my life."

Cohen caressed his daughter's face. "But the semester just started."

"I'm not saying I'm dropping out. I just don't have to start another semester." Hannah seemed a bit flustered. "Listen, you're smart. If the business fails, I'm sure you won't have any trouble finding a job. Just don't worry about me, okay?"

"But it's my responsibility to look after you."

"I'm saying don't let my college be part of your burden. We'll figure it out together." They stood and hugged.

Cohen's back was to me, but I could see the love radiating from Hannah's face. I couldn't remember ever loving my father like that.

Chapter Eleven

"[F]or he who doubts is like a wave of the sea driven and tossed by the wind." James 1:6b NKJV

Dusk descended around six o'clock, made luminescent by the falling snow. It lent an eeriness to the atmosphere in the church.

Cohen kissed Hannah on the forehead, then glanced at his watch as they parted from their hug. Only 6:40. He strode to a window. What did he expect to see in Nowhere, Nebraska—or South Dakota? It didn't matter. Certainly neither would boast any street lights. But as he stared blankly out into the blackness, he realized the burden of his business had left him. *The business may fail, but that doesn't make you a failure.* Abby's words brought a salve to his soul. He sighed audibly.

"What's it look like out there?" Abby asked, entering from the kitchen. "I brought some more ice for your wrist."

Cohen turned away from the window. "It's too dark to even see if it's still snowing."

"Here." Hannah grabbed the lantern from off the table. "Let's try holding the lamp up to the window." She walked over. Both peered out into the bleak night. Cohen cupped his left hand around his eyes to shut out the light from the room, hoping to see better outside.

"Well?" Abby asked after a long silence.

"Still snowing, as far as I can tell. Hannah, what about you?" He looked at her with expectancy.

"Yeah, still snowing."

"Getting to Rapid City isn't going to happen tonight or tomorrow." He pulled out his cell phone and checked for a signal. "Blast, still no signal."

"Time to consider switching carriers?" Sally said.

Did she say that just to goad him? "Abby, you had a signal on your cell phone earlier. Do you have one now? I've got to call the conference organizer and let him know there's no way I can be there in the morning." After the way he'd behaved earlier, he wasn't sure she would be willing to let him use her phone.

Abby pulled her cell from her purse and checked it. "You're in luck." She handed him the phone. "First, let me put this ice pack on your wrist."

"I apologize for getting angry earlier. I was way out of line." He gave her a weak smile of thanks, then winced a bit as she placed the ice.

"Would you like some pain reliever? I think Sally has some in her purse."

"Maybe later, but thanks." He grabbed a lamp and walked to the kitchen to gain some privacy. He dialed the number and waited for an answer.

"Hello?"

"Tom? It's Cohen."

"I almost didn't answer. Didn't recognize the number. Where're you at?"

"Snowed in at a little country church about an hour from Rapid City. I'm sorry, but there's no way I can get there tonight or tomorrow. We've been stuck at this church since two o' clock. Even if the storm ended and the crews got the road plowed, I couldn't make it. I crashed into a ditch. Once things do clear up, I'll be calling for a tow truck."

"Crashed? Are you and Hannah all right? Are you warm? Do you have food and water?"

"Yeah, yeah, we're fine. Only thing missing from supper was dessert. And somehow I think if we'd asked for that, we'd find it."

"What?"

"Never mind. This place is…I don't know. Just weird. As for tomorrow, Tom, can you pinch hit for me?"

"Might not have to. A lot of registrants have called and canceled. Everyone is having the same problem with the snow. The airport had shut down, but did manage to reopen."

"Yeah, George told me that earlier today. I called not long after getting stranded. He was none too happy."

"Don't sweat it. That's George for you. The conference committee is still mulling over whether to cancel, postpone, or go ahead. I should have their decision in the next half hour. I'll send out an email to everyone as soon as I find out. Those who live in Rapid City will probably be fine, but the majority of our attendees are from out of town."

"How much snow have you had there?" Cohen asked.

"Around eight inches at my house, but it varies throughout the region. The weatherman is reporting six. It's stopped snowing here, but it's still overcast."

"It's still snowing here as far as we can tell. It's pitch black outside." Cohen took a deep breath and plunged forward. "Look, I blew my top at George earlier. He kept insisting I pay back the advance fee. I was counting on gaining new clients at this conference. I really need the work." He and Tom had been friends for more than a decade. In fact, Tom had helped Cohen set up his consulting business and been a mentor for his first two years as an entrepreneur.

"Talk to me. What's going on?"

"I don't know. No matter how much time I spend at the office, the clients keep dropping and new ones are non-existent. If things don't change soon, I'm in real trouble."

"Why haven't you called to talk things through? I might have been able to help somehow."

"I thought things would turn around, that this conference…that's not going to happen. Right now, I just want to get out of this place and get home."

"I don't want to add to your burden, but George is probably right about the advance fee."

"I can't pay 'em what I haven't got." He'd have to come up with the money somehow.

"It's that bad?"

"It's that bad, but I'll figure something out. Good night, Tom. I'll call you when I get back home." Cohen clicked off the phone before Tom could mount an argument. He stood staring out into the black night, yet searching deep into his soul. He felt as empty as the blackness staring back at him.

He mulled over more of Abby's words from earlier. *You've turned your back on God because your business is failing.* Cohen chortled. *Turned my back on God?* Abby's words grated on his soul. If he was honest with himself, he'd have to admit he'd never had any real faith to begin with. Plenty of head knowledge, but faith? Probably not.

He made his way back into the sanctuary. Reverend Salem had returned, apparently finished with his prayers.

"Cohen, I'm glad you're back," Reverend Salem said. "While we still have some energy left, let's arrange pews around the stove so we can all benefit from its warmth throughout the night."

"I can't manage with my wrist." Cohen lifted his injured wing. He handed Abby her phone. "Thanks."

"I'll help, Reverend," Hannah said. She and the reverend busied themselves arranging five pews around the stove, transforming the little church into an indoor campground. It reminded Cohen of the last camping trip the family had taken. How long ago was that? Hannah hadn't even started kindergarten. Where had all the years disappeared to?

While the next hour ticked by, he watched as, one by one, first Hannah, then Abby, then Sally grabbed a blanket from near the stove and settled into a pew for the night. Reverend Salem sat in the pew next to Sally's, his eyes closed, his lips moving but silent. Probably praying, Cohen thought with exasperation.

He might as well call it night too. What else was there to do? He grabbed a blanket, sat down on the pew next to Hannah's, and observed the room a bit longer. With only the light of one small hurricane lamp and the firelight filtering through the stove grate, he was unable to see the burned half of the church.

He stood and gave Hannah a peck on the forehead. "Good night."

"Good night, Dad. Sleep well."

"That's anyone's guess. I've never slept on a church pew before."

"I'm glad I'm not shivering to death in the car," Hannah said.

"You're right. You're very mature for your age." He gave her another quick kiss on the forehead. "Don't let the bed bugs bite, pumpkin."

Hannah smiled up at him. "You haven't called me that in ages. I love you, Dad." She hugged his neck.

Cohen returned to his pew, pushed off his shoes, then attempted to get comfortable. "How 'bout you, Reverend? You gonna stay up all night praying?" He wondered if his voice carried the cynicism he felt.

"I might."

"Sorry. Guess it's really none of my business what you do." Cohen stretched out, but with his arm in a sling and his wrist pulsing with pain, he struggled to get comfortable. He preferred to sleep on his right side. As he lay there on his back, staring at the ceiling, he rehearsed the day's events in his head.

Plowed the car into a ditch. Sprained, maybe broke, my wrist. Found a half-burned church to take refuge in. Church populated with a crazy woman Marine, her twin sister, and a persistent preacher. Can't get to the conference. Gotta pay back the advance fee. My business is failing. And I'm about to go bankrupt.

Would God provide a way through like Abby said He would?

He rubbed his left hand through his hair and turned to face the pew. Now he felt like everyone was staring at his back. He quickly rolled over. Joshua had lain down, but it was hard to tell if he was asleep. Hannah's closed eyes and rhythmic breathing told him she was. Abby and Sally both appeared asleep as well.

Man, it's gonna be a long night.

Chapter Twelve

"Even at night my heart instructs me." Psalm 16:7b NLT

Sally, yer mother is gone, stop yer cryin'. Yer worthless, good for nothing. Ain't no daughter of mine...Worthless, good for nothing. Ain't no daughter of mine...You're ugly. Ain't no one who wants you." Smack!

But I didn't feel a thing.

I noticed a drop of red on my shirt and then another and another.

I watched, paralyzed, as blood saturated my shirt.

Yet I didn't feel anything.

I didn't feel a thing.

Not a thing.

I woke with a start, nearly falling off the pew. I drew in a long deep breath and forcefully blew it out, hoping to blow away my nightmare. Eight years of hearing those words and enduring his slaps. Would my father's words forever taunt and haunt me? And why all that bleeding yet feeling nothing? I mulled that over for several minutes, and then the answer struck me. My father's words had been like a bullet to my heart, yet I had grown oblivious to the pain they still inflicted. Until I grappled with that pain and conquered it, the life I wanted would continue to bleed away.

I pulled the blanket over my shoulders and tried to go back to sleep, but the scenes kept replaying themselves. Like my computer trying unsuccessfully to load a web page, my brain failed to load a new file.

"Worthless…ain't no daughter of mine…You're ugly. Ain't no one wants you." With every word my shirt grew redder and redder.

I squeezed my eyes tighter and shook my head in an effort to jog the file.

"Ain't no one wants you…no one…no one—"

"Stop!" I bolted up in the pew. Apparently, I had fallen back to sleep only to dream the same dreadful nightmare again. Thankfully it was only sweat dribbling down my chest and not blood. I rubbed my hand across my shirt to dry the sweat and wiped the moisture from my upper lip. To clear my head and the pounding in my ears, I focused on my breathing.

Someone had extinguished the hurricane lamp, but the glow from the grate of the stove cast a deep pumpkin hue across the room. Had my outburst wakened anyone? I scrutinized each person-occupied pew. No one stirred, but the light snoring I'd heard moments earlier had ceased.

Here I was again, in the dark…in a strange place…in the wee hours of the morning, my mind whirling with questions. At least this time I wasn't in the hospital recovering from a rattlesnake bite. I stood, wrapped the blanket around me, and tiptoed to my suitcase. I pulled out my e-reader and made my way to the front of the church. Once there, I sat next to the wooden cross that stood to the left of the stained-glass window, turned on my e-reader, and waited for it to boot up. I would read my favorite psalm, Psalm 16. That should calm my nerves and chase away my father's hateful words.

But after reading it three times through, my father's voice had gotten louder. I put the e-reader to sleep and laid it next to me.

"No weapon formed against me shall prosper," I whispered. "That voice is lying to me. I am a child of God, made in His image. God delights in me. I have been given authority to trample on snakes and scorpions and over all the power of the enemy. Nothing shall injure me. God, I submit to you. Satan, I resist you and your demons; you must flee." I began to pray in the Spirit and immediately the jeering voice in my head stopped.

"I've struggled all my life to prove my father's words aren't true. God, how do I silence them forever?" I whispered.

You must first stop believing those words.

I thought about that for a moment. If I knew something was a lie, would I be so upset about it? Would I have a need to prove it wasn't true? But my father attacked my very identity. If I wasn't his daughter, whose daughter was I and why had they abandoned me?

Your parents did not abandon you.

"I know that now, God, but not while I was growing up. I...I hold onto my identity as a Marine because it's the one place I felt I did belong."

You are My daughter, and you belong to My kingdom. You've repeated your father's words so often because you did believe them. Now bitterness has taken root. You've stayed angry at him because it motivated you to conquer his abuse. You've used that anger as a tool to conquer every challenge in your life.

"Are you serious, God? How have I done that?"

Don't you remember what you said each night for months as you cried yourself to sleep after your mother died?

I searched my memories but came up empty. "No, I don't, God. But I'm sure You do."

My mommy loved me. I don't care if my father doesn't. I'll hate him like he hates me.

At those words, childhood memories flooded me, nearly drowning me in the raw grief I felt those first few months after Mom's death. A motion picture reel of the following years of my life revealed how I had projected that same hate onto nearly every boy and man I met, especially those who had shown any romantic interest in me. Bitterness strangled my soul.

"Oh, God, I'm so sorry," I sobbed. "What do I do now?

Forgive your father.

"I have forgiven, over and over and over."

You wouldn't even speak to your father.

"By avoiding him, I avoided the pain he inflicted with every word and every slap from his hand. I needed that boundary. Was I supposed to let him keep hurting me?"

Once you left home you could have at least written him.

"What good would writing have done?"

It would have opened the door to healing.

"Healing?"

Nothing is impossible for Me.

"Well, I screwed that up, and now, it's too late."

But there's no expiration date on forgiveness. Do you want to live a life as bitter as his was?

"No! I…I want to enjoy the abundant life Jesus died to give me."

Then you must learn to forgive all those who have hurt you, past, present, and future.

"You don't ask much, do You?"

Have I asked you to do anything I have not already done for you?

"I know. I know. I'm sorry. I don't mean to argue or be rude. Like King David did as he wrote his psalms, I'm being honest. You know what I'm thinking, but it helps me to say it."

Remember forgiveness means you let go of offenses and stop demanding justice for them. When you don't forgive, your heart holds things it was not created to hold.

As I focused on God, my anger and frustration slowly melted away. A sense of peace permeated my spirit, leaving me refreshed as though I sat beside a gentle brook with the warmth of the summer sun on my skin. Worship came as a natural response. I don't know how long I worshiped before silent tears began to spill down my cheeks.

"Abby was right. All that bitterness is spewing out on those around me. I don't want that. Jesus, help me let go of these wounds and forgive those who've hurt me. Heal my heart." I wiped my tears with the corner of the blanket and continued praying until the chill in the air drove me back to the warmth of the stove. I put my e-reader back in my suitcase, and as I curled up on my pew, I heard snoring from more than one person. I was glad the others could sleep.

"I will trust in You, Lord," I whispered as I settled myself.

Don't be afraid, for I am with you. Don't be discouraged, for I am your God. I will strengthen you and help you. I will hold you up with my victorious right hand.

I took a deep breath and let it out slowly. I seemed to be doing that a lot lately. "I love you, Abba. Thank You for taking care of me in the midst of this snowstorm. I know You'll see me through all my storms. 'For You alone are my safe place.'"

I took one more calming breath and consciously relaxed my body as I exhaled. What would it take to let go of forty-some years of anger? How was I going to root out the unforgiveness and bitterness in my heart? Had I been sabotaging myself all these years by unconsciously pushing away every man who ever showed an interest in me? Did I have so few friends because I expected the worst from everybody? Worse yet, did I get the worst from everyone because that's what I expected? Self-fulfilling prophecy, as they say.

What would my life be like if I started expecting good things from people? It was time for change.

Chapter Thirteen

"And lean not on your own understanding." Proverbs 3:5b NKJV

"Stop!"

Cohen's eyes popped open at the outburst. In the pew directly across the circle, sat Sally. She must have had a bad dream, but he had barely fallen asleep. He closed his eyes, hoping to get back to sleep without any trouble. When he heard her stirring, he opened his eyes again. From his vantage point, he could see her tiptoe to her suitcase, pull something out of it, then tiptoe to the front of the church. She sat in the corner and leaned against the wall.

He glanced over at Hannah, then at Abby. Both still sleeping. Good. He shifted his attention back to Sally. Her back was facing him, but he continued to watch anyway. A glow of white light illuminated her face. She must have an iPad or something she was looking at. After several minutes she turned it off and set it down. He could hear her whispering. Who was she talking to? Herself? More proof she was crazy.

Several minutes passed when he noticed her shoulders jerking as though she was crying. He took some small pleasure in her present discomfort. She wiped her eyes with the blanket. Where was her God now?

Cohen watched her for another twenty minutes, then feigned sleep when she rose and returned to her pew.

"I trust You, Lord," he heard her whisper. "I love you, Abba. Thank you for taking care of me in the midst of this snowstorm. I know You'll see me through all my storms. For You alone are my safe place."

Abba? Who was that? And how was this Abba caring for her in this snowstorm? Did she mean God? They were all stranded for who knew how long in the middle of these desolate plains. How could she lie there and say "I trust you, Lord"?

The Bible verse Rev had quoted earlier in the evening drifted through Cohen's thoughts. Something about God causing everything to work for good.

Humph! His business was nearly dead, and he was going bankrupt. How was any of that good? Besides that verse had qualifiers to it—you had to love God and be called.

You've gotten lost along the way. More of Rev's earlier words echoed in Cohen's head.

Rev told him he *was* called. But called for what? And how had he gotten lost?

The reverend's pew sat empty. Cohen scanned the room. No sign of him anywhere. Cohen marveled at the darkness that enveloped the room. Yet the meager light from the stove seemed to penetrate the darkness in an unusual way.

He listened for the wind. Every now and then he could hear it whistle through the cracks somewhere in the building. Probably still snowing too. No more Rapid City. No more convention. How was he going to pay back that advance? How could the conference committee demand it when the circumstances were beyond his control?

He rubbed his eyes in an effort to wipe away all those thoughts. He wasn't going to solve anything from the discomfort of this pew. Things would look better in the morning. The snow will have stopped, the plows would be out, and they would get out of here.

His gut ached. His wrist throbbed. Emptiness reigned in his heart.

The crash of glass startled Cohen awake. He jolted up in his pew; all the others did too. As one, they turned toward the sound and watched a branch crash through a window and to the floor. Glass and bits of wood debris scattered across the floor. With the ferocity of a grizzly bear, the bitter cold, the howling wind, and snow once again invaded the secure coziness of their sanctuary.

Cohen stared over at the window. The sound of breaking glass had clearly resounded in his ears, but all the windows on that side of the church were boarded over. What glass had broken? He flung off his blanket and quickly slipped his feet into his shoes. The reverend was busy doing the same. They each rushed toward the window. Hannah, Abby, and Sally followed closely behind, each with her blanket wrapped tightly around her. For several seconds they all stood shocked, staring at the mess on the floor, the snow blowing in and whirling its icy fingers around them. Could things get any worse? He needed to quit asking himself that question.

Cohen scanned the floor for boards, certain he'd find the large piece of plywood the tree branch had knocked loose from the window. Nothing. Only fragments of glass and the large branch.

"Reverend, have you got any boards we can nail up over this window?" he hollered above the howl of the wind.

"I'm not sure. In the basement maybe." The reverend rushed off.

"Hannah, watch out for that glass!" Sally warned. "Would you go to the kitchen and see if you can find a broom, a dust pan, and a trash can? Take my flashlight; it's under my pew."

Hannah glanced at Cohen for approval. He nodded, and she dutifully obeyed, slipping on her jacket before dashing off to the kitchen.

"Abby, let's move this branch out of the way," Sally said.

They each took one end of the large branch and carried it to the back of the church, then hurried back and began piling bits of branches and the larger pieces of glass out of the way.

"I could have sworn all four of these windows were boarded over. Where did all this glass come from?" Cohen said while they worked.

Sally stood straight and observed the wall. "Four boarded windows? None of those windows is—" She shook her head as she stood staring at the windows. "I'm certain none of those were boarded yesterday. Now I see one boarded, but not the other three."

"No, all of them are boarded over," Cohen insisted. About that time Hannah returned with a broom and trash barrel. Abby took the broom and began sweeping the glass from the wood floor as best she could. Hannah and Sally picked up bits of wood from the window frame, twigs, and the larger pieces of glass and tossed them into the trash.

"It was so nice and toasty in here. Now it'll take forever to warm up again." Hannah's shoulders shuddered from the cold and snow gusting in. Abby stopped sweeping long enough to grab her coat and put it on.

"Wait a minute, Hannah. Let's save the twigs and wood for the stove." Sally dove into the twenty-gallon trash barrel to snatch what they'd already thrown in. "Let's hope Joshua can find some boards. We could put a blanket over the window to keep out most of the snow, but that certainly won't do much to stop the cold."

"I'm sure he'll find what's needed." No sooner had Abby spoken than Reverend Salem returned carrying several boards. He dropped them on the floor with a bang.

"Cohen, come help me," Reverend Salem said. They left the room. A minute or so later, Cohen returned with hammer and nails in hand, the reverend right behind him with a ladder.

For several minutes only the sound of the wind and banging of boards penetrated the peace that once ruled the little sanctuary. Sally continued picking up pieces of glass and tree. Her brow crinkled and a deep frown crossed her lips, apparently stunned at the revelation of the boarded window.

"Hannah, why don't you make some fresh coffee and start it brewing on the stove," Abby suggested. "And some hot chocolate for yourself."

"That sounds good." Hannah scurried to the kitchen, a smile on her face.

"I—I just don't recall that window being boarded," Sally said. "Abby, were any of the windows boarded when we got here?"

"No, I'm as sure of that as you are. Honestly, Sally, I don't see any of them boarded even now."

Cohen harrumphed as he handed the reverend a board. "I told you yesterday when we got here there were four boarded windows and the place looked like it had been in a fire."

"Cohen, I'm going to need help holding these boards in place," Rev said. "Let's work from the bottom up, so each board can rest on the one below it. That should keep them straight and relieve some of the burden of holding them in place. I'll need the ladder. Grab a chair from over at the table so you have something to stand on."

Cohen quickly retrieved a chair.

"I can't understand why you see things so much differently than I do," Cohen said to Abby as he climbed onto the chair.

"I suppose because Sally and I have a different perspective than you. And it's a good thing we do. We've got heat. When you insisted that stove was cold, Sally insisted otherwise. And who was right? I prayed for God to provide a safe place for us to weather the storm, and He answered my prayer. We see with the eyes of our faith. You see with your natural eyes."

Cohen started laughing. "Faith! Faith never got me anywhere!"

"God's answers to our prayers are all about His covenant with Jesus—" Reverend Salem started to say.

"Enough! I don't want to hear it," Cohen yelled. "Just hurry up and get that board nailed; with only one hand, I don't know how much longer I can hold it in place against this wind."

"Sally, why don't you take Cohen's place?" Reverend Salem finished nailing the board in place, then Cohen stepped down and Sally stepped up.

They all worked in silence from there on, with heads down.

Cohen grumbled to himself as he picked up bits of twigs and glass and tossed them into the trash. These people were crazy. Or was he? If he was dead and this was hell, he never imagined it like this.

Chapter Fourteen

"LORD, you alone are my inheritance." Psalm 16:5a NLT

I prayed in the Spirit as Joshua positioned one board after another and nailed it in place. That one boarded window confounded me. I stared at it time and again, shaking my head and determining to talk to Joshua about it later.

The broken window finally boarded, we all heaved a deep sigh and retreated to the warmth of the stove and a hot cup of coffee. Hannah cautiously sipped hot chocolate.

I grabbed a small pile of the twigs we had just gathered and tossed them into the stove. The fire sizzled as it met with the ice coated twigs.

"Oh boy, I hope I didn't just mess up the fire."

"Wood is best for burning if it's seasoned first. I don't know if that tree is green or dead. Let's avoid the twigs unless we run out of everything else," Joshua said. "I'll see if I can find another blanket. We can put it up over the boards to curtail the wind and snow invading through the small cracks that still exist." He headed to the basement.

Goodness knows how far-reaching this storm was and what the highways looked like between here and Rapid City, or Scottsbluff for that matter. I picked up my phone from under my pew. It read 3:30, and my battery power was at 39 percent. Blast! I should have switched it off yesterday.

"Hey, everybody, if your phone is still turned on, switch it off to conserve the battery," I hollered out to no one in particular. I tapped my phone's weather app. Nineteen degrees with a wind chill of six below, and snow forecast through tomorrow—today—before the sun appeared again. I kept this tidbit of news to myself. Sure didn't want to make Cohen more worried, nor did I need to listen to his complaints. I powered off my phone and laid it back under my pew.

We were halfway to Rapid City, only ninety miles away, yet it might as well have been a thousand. God, what the devil has intended for evil, I know You will turn for good. Help me to keep my eyes on You and not this storm.

Joshua returned with a blanket and I helped him cover the boarded window. I tucked the edges of the blanket under the boards as best I could to block the snow and air from getting in. Joshua added some nails along each edge of the blanket.

"Now that we've got that done, let's try to go back to sleep," Joshua said.

"You kidding? That branch crashing through the window triggered my fight or flight response. For a moment I was back in the Middle East," I said. "My adrenaline needs to dissipate first." I nabbed my e-reader, switched it on, and walked back to my pew and lay down. Everyone attempted to get comfortable on their own pew. "Good night again, everyone," I said.

I heard a good night from everyone except Cohen.

When day two of our forced confinement dawned, the storm raged on just as the weatherman had forecast. I turned my phone on long enough to catch the time: 7:30. Surely the sun had risen by now, but as dark as the sanctuary was, it was hard to tell. I trekked to the south window and looked out. Nothing but white greeted me. Not good, but not a surprise. Actually, conditions seemed worse than yesterday's.

I grabbed my flashlight and made my way to the restroom in the basement. That done, I grabbed the coffee pot from the stove and went to the kitchen to make fresh coffee. I also cleaned the pot we'd been using to make hot chocolate for Hannah. While the coffee boiled, I grabbed my Bible from my suitcase and sat down to read while everyone else was still asleep.

The world sat eerily quiet, the snow having dampened all sound. For the time being, even the howl of the wind had disappeared. I tried to read the psalms, but my mind kept distracting me. Why hadn't I checked the weather before we started on our way to Rapid City? For that matter, why had I so readily accepted the invitation from Abby to visit the Reynolds? And to stay so long? What was I thinking when I agreed to that?

Perhaps my time in Montana would allow me to work through my current dilemma. My substantial inheritance from Chase Reynolds, Jr. opened the door to starting a company of my own, being a full-time author, or living a life of leisure from now on. As appealing as a life of leisure is to many people, sitting around doing nothing didn't appeal to me. Yet, I didn't have peace about the other two options either.

I shook my head and asked the Holy Spirit to help me focus on my reading. As I was turning to Psalm 21, my eye caught the word *inheritance* in Psalm 16. I decided to read that.

"Keep me safe, O God, for I have come to you for refuge. I said to the LORD, 'You are my Master! Every good thing I have comes from you.' ... LORD, you alone are my inheritance, my cup of blessing. You guard all that is mine. The land you have given me is a pleasant land."

A thought was on the verge of my mind when a gust of wind made the church shudder and creak, startling me out of my communion with God. The noise must have awakened Joshua. I watched as he rose, grabbed a lamp, and left the room. I closed my Bible and set it under the pew.

The wail of the wind returned like a banshee, setting my nerves on edge. I clambered to the stove in an attempt to ward off the cold that seemed to penetrate me with every wail. Except for Joshua, everyone else still lay nestled under their blankets on their pews. Joshua hadn't returned to the sanctuary. He had probably retreated to his office.

Cohen stretched and looked around the room, then bolted up off the pew and rushed to the window. What did he expect to find? The sun shining brilliantly on the night's freshly fallen snow? His shoulders fell as he looked out into an arctic expanse of snow still furiously falling.

"When will this end?" he muttered.

I heard some morning groans and yawns and knew the others were waking. Cohen turned away from the window and headed back to his pew. "It's like we moved to Antarctica. Can't see two feet beyond the window. Nothing but white."

"I'm so thankful we have this bit of sanctuary in this storm," Abby said. "I can't imagine being stuck in the car all this time."

"We'd be dead. Frozen," Hannah said from her prone position on her pew.

"Don't be melodramatic, Hannah," Cohen said. "I'd have run the heat in the car, and our body heat would have helped keep us warm."

"Maybe so, Dad. But you don't know how cold it got last night. If the temperature fell below zero, we'd have been shivering most of the night. And who knows how long this storm will last. We didn't have water or food in the car. No winter emergency kit with blankets or stuff like that."

"All right, point taken. We're here and we're safe."

"Praise God for that," I said.

"How did everybody sleep?" Abby asked. "I think we'd better stoke the fire." She grabbed a hot pad, opened the stove door, and peered in, then shoved three logs in one by one.

"Thank you for doing that, Abby." Joshua entered the sanctuary.

She sent him a smile.

"Sleeping on this pew sure didn't agreed with me," Hannah said, cautiously sitting up. I watched as she rolled her head around as if attempting to loosen her neck muscles. "My neck is stiff and my head hurts."

"I've got ibuprofen and Tylenol if you'd like some pain killer," I told Hannah.

"Yes, thank you," she said.

I headed to my purse and grabbed my pill container.

"Are you half boy scout or something? You seem prepared for anything," Cohen snapped. He stood and went over to Hannah. "Can I rub your neck or shoulders? Would that help?"

"No, but thanks for offering, Dad."

"Being in the Marine Corps for fifteen years taught me how to be prepared. Besides, a migraine can warn me at any time that it's on its way. As long as I take something before the pain hits, I can thwart the migraine altogether, so I've learned to always carry pain killer with me," I explained.

"It warns you? How's that?" Hannah asked.

"I get what's called an aura, little lights flashing in one eye." I looked down at the pan of chocolate milk. "The coffee and hot chocolate are ready. Does everyone like scrambled eggs? I'd be glad to cook breakfast."

"That sounds yummy." Hannah rose from her mock bed, stretched, and trudged off to the bathroom. I removed the hot chocolate and coffee from the stove and placed them each on a hot pad on the table. Then Abby and I bustled to the kitchen and started breakfast.

As I whipped ten eggs, the wind whipped the snow outside. That feeling of being adrift washed over me again. All my years at Pendrake Publishing gone. And whose fault was that? Mine. I'd quit my job as an editor to go to Montana to claim my inheritance. But my job had become almost unbearable, so quitting wasn't hard. Berkeley Snyder had tried to woo me back by enticing me with heading up an imprint for Christian fiction. But I had declined that, and they had declined my offer to buy the company.

Now my best friend, Jennifer Maxwell, and I could start our own publishing company. The thought did spark a bit of excitement in me. But now that her husband had the opportunity to become a partner in the law firm he worked for, even starting a business with Jen was in jeopardy.

God, what do I do now?

Enjoy the day.

Enjoy the day? Not exactly the answer I expected. I'd spent the majority of my life working to survive. Did I know how to enjoy anything?

I guess I did. I'd visited most of Europe during my time in the Corps. I didn't have a bucket list, but if I did, visiting New Zealand would be on it.

I turned my attention back to the task at hand. I grated some cheese; Abby chopped some onion. I dumped them both into the bowl of scrambled eggs, and we returned to the sanctuary to cook.

While I stirred the eggs, I watched Cohen pace around the church. He looked at his watch and shrugged. I suppose if he hadn't gotten stuck here, he'd be getting ready to address that conference in Rapid City. The situation was out of his control. Had the conference organizers canceled, postponed the event, or moved forward?

I hummed one of my favorite songs and continued cooking. A quizzical look crossed Cohen's face, then he clenched his jaw.

"How can you sing 'Amazing Grace' at a time like this?"

I chortled. "I'm surprised you know the song."

"Why are you constantly snapping at Sally?" Abby asked.

"What do you mean?" Cohen stopped his pacing.

"I mean that nearly every word you direct to Sally is angry or rude. Why? You don't speak to me that way."

Cohen shrugged. "I guess we got off on the wrong foot when I first got here and she insisted the stove was hot. And she seems to have an answer for everything."

"No I don't have an answer for everything. I have faith in God to take care of us."

"Cohen, God's grace is amazing." Abby walked to a window. "Sally and I could be stuck in the snow somewhere"—she pointed outside—"half-frozen or dead by now if God hadn't shown us this church. You could be too. What He does in our lives is amazing, whether you notice it or not."

That seemed to shut him up and he returned to his pacing.

###

After eating breakfast and washing the dishes, I checked my phone for a signal. Nothing. Then how had I been able to access my weather app last night? Maybe I should take my own advice and change carriers, but I suppose it was anybody's guess how the storm affected cell towers. I dialed 911 anyway, hoping the call would somehow connect.

"911, what is your emergency?"

"Oh, wow, I had no signal on my phone and didn't know if I'd get anybody."

"Your phone is connecting to another service provider, ma'am. What is your location?"

"We're at Christ Community Church, a few miles north of Ardmore, South Dakota. I know there's probably nothing you can do now, not with this storm still buffeting the region, but I wanted someone to know there are five of us stranded by this storm."

"Is anyone hurt?" the 911 operator asked.

"One man has a sprained, possibly broken wrist, but everyone else seems fine. We're safe for now."

"Ardmore is nothing but a ghost town these days. I can't imagine any building solid enough to offer protection. Is the structure sound? Do you have power?"

"The building is old, but solid. The power went out yesterday afternoon."

"Are you able to stay warm?"

"Yeah, there's a wood-burning stove, and it's doing a good job of keeping us warm. There's also plenty of food and water."

"So everyone is in relatively good health and safe?" the operator asked.

"Yes. I just felt it was important for someone to know we were here. I mean, the storm is forecast to last at least through today and who knows how long it will take to get the roads cleared after that."

"Yes, ma'am. I understand. Hwy 71 is rarely traveled and is the last of the roads cleared. Snowplows will clear main highways first, so it could be one to two days after the storm ends before that road gets cleared."

"Guess that's what I get for choosing the scenic route."

"Ma'am, I've noted your situation and the information will be passed onto the next shift 911 supervisor and to the supervisor on the street. Your situation will be tracked. If conditions should worsen considerably, call back. It is possible for police or fire fighters to drive out as far as they can get and then by ATV to execute a rescue. The closest town with emergency services is twenty-seven miles from Ardmore. In these conditions, that might take several hours."

"All the same, it's comforting to know we can reach 911 and get help if needed. Thank you so much." The closest help was twenty-seven miles away? I'd better not let Cohen know that fact.

"Rest assured, ma'am, we'll do all we can make sure you're safe."

"Thank you. Goodbye." I clicked off the call, powered off my phone, and returned to our little group in the sanctuary. Everyone was warming themselves around the stove.

"Hey, gang. I just spoke to a 911 operator about our situation. They're aware we're here. I told her we're all safe, warm, and fed, so for now they are simply keeping track of us. If things get worse somehow, all we have to do is call back."

"Well, that's a relief," Hannah said.

"Wait a minute! You got through to 911 and told them we didn't need help?" Cohen growled.

"That's right. Because we're safe and healthy." I glared at him. He stared back, his eyes squinting as he did so. Was that his impression of the evil eye?

"My wrist is possibly broken, yet you took it upon yourself to decide we didn't need help?"

"Why tie up important resources when others who are seriously injured or stranded in the elements truly need help? I didn't think—"

"No, you didn't *think!*" Cohen's face turned red and a vein along his neck bulged to the surface. "You didn't think to ask us how we felt. Do me a favor. Don't think for me."

"Well pardon me. Call them back, if you want."

"We tried calling 911 when I first plowed into that ditch. The call never went through; it was just dead air. How did *you* get through?"

If there had been something handy to throw, he probably would have thrown it.

"Dad, we're safe. That's all that matters." Hannah sent Cohen a look he appeared to understand even if I didn't. "Neither one of us needs urgent medical care. Abby's been managing first aid just fine."

That seemed to calm him down, and he retreated to his favorite window.

Chapter Fifteen

"Choose for yourselves this day whom you
will serve." Joshua 24:15b NKJV

Cohen stood staring out the window. If they had made it to Rapid
City, he'd have enjoyed a workout in the hotel fitness room and
a hot shower this morning in preparation for the conference. He
felt kind of grungy after last night's work boarding the window. He
wondered if the conference had been canceled or postponed. If postponed, at least he wouldn't have to pay back the advance fee because
he'd still be speaking. But canceled? The situation was out of his control. He'd manage some way to pay back the advance.

He absentmindedly rubbed his aching wrist as he glanced around
the room. It appeared everyone was reading something. Sally lounged
on a pew. Man, that women grated his nerves. She had the same answer
for everything: God will provide. Yeah, right. God certainly hadn't provided for him.

He began to pace the room. If he was stuck in this place too long, he'd
go crazy. He decided he'd explore the church. He hadn't ventured anywhere outside the sanctuary except to the restroom. And yesterday, he
had only poked his head into the kitchen. He'd start there. He followed
the hallway past the basement stairway and to the kitchen. A large window over the sink offered all the light he needed to observe the room.

"Humph! Look at this place. It's like stepping back into the 1940s.
That refrigerator is an antique!" He ventured over, pulled the handle,

139

and peered inside, half expecting cobwebs. No cobwebs, but dark and empty. He shut the door and turned away, then abruptly stopped. He turned back to the refrigerator, his hand on the door pull. He hesitated, looking around for another refrigerator, but found none. Hannah had been drinking hot chocolate made from milk, not an instant powder. Yesterday afternoon they'd eaten cheese sandwiches and tomato soup made with milk. Bratwurst last night and scrambled eggs this morning. All those things needed to be kept cold. If that antique was empty, where were Sally and Abby getting the food they made for every meal?

He closed his eyes and pulled the door open again. He slowly opened one eye. The light was on, shining out across a carton of milk, several dozen eggs, packages of Velveeta cheese slices, a bag of carrots and other various vegetables, along with a couple loaves of bread. He haltingly stepped backwards, his breath whooshing out. His mouth agape, he closed his eyes again. "This is not happening. This is not happening." He opened his eyes. The GE stood shining brightly out at him. He slammed the door and went in search of the reverend.

He made his way back down the hall to the stairway. The temperature grew consistently cooler with each step down the stairs, and the darkness deepened. He should have grabbed a flashlight or one of the hurricane lamps. The stairway T-ed at a small hallway. He turned left and found what appeared to be the utility room. He could just make out the shape of a furnace and a water heater. He turned around and went back the other way. He passed the restroom and continued.

At the end of the hallway was what appeared to be an office. Two glass block windows shed enough light into the room for him to make out a desk, a bookshelf, and a wardrobe. Cobwebs hung everywhere, and he could only guess at how thick the dust was. None of this made sense.

Cohen peered down the hallway. A bathroom, a utility room, and an office. This had to be the reverend's office, but how could it be? And where was the reverend? He let his head drop and rubbed his aching wrist. He stood there like that for several seconds. He looked up again at the dusty forsaken room, shook his head, and started back down the hallway to the stairs.

"Did you need something, Cohen?"

Startled at the man's voice behind him, he whirled around to face him. It was Reverend Salem. Cohen stepped toward him and glanced back into the room, now dust and cobweb free and lit with a hurricane lamp.

"How...this...man, I must be going crazy." He stared at Reverend Salem. "A moment ago only vacant furniture, cobwebs, and dust filled this room. Now...I'm just imagining things."

"I suppose the conditions we're facing can wreak havoc on one's mind," Reverend Salem said. "But I doubt you're going crazy. You've been working too hard. Take advantage of this down time to relax. It's not good for your body to be stressed out all the time."

"Relax! How can I relax when my business is failing and I'm stuck here instead of being at that conference?"

"Making that conference was no guarantee you were going to gain new clients," the reverend said calmly.

Cohen glared at him. Talking to Rev was as exasperating as talking to Sally. "Just forget it!" He turned and stomped back upstairs to the sanctuary and plopped down in a pew. His wrist throbbed. His head ached. Nothing made sense and hadn't since he and Hannah had entered this strange little church. As much as he hated to, he asked Sally for some ibuprofen and swilled them down with his now-tepid cup of coffee.

The morning dragged on. He couldn't even twiddle his thumbs; it was too painful. The ibuprofen helped, but certain movements shot pain up his arm. He found some ice in the ancient refrigerator, iced his wrist, and wiggled his toes instead.

Around noon, Hannah, Abby, and Sally started some lunch, and the reverend returned from his office.

"Hey, wait a minute!" Sally whirled around from her lunch task at the pot-bellied stove and faced Cohen. "Yesterday you insisted there were four boarded windows on that side of the church. So how do you explain that one of those *boarded* windows shattered glass all over the place last night when that branch came crashing through it?"

He turned to the windows and examined them. Four boarded windows. Sally was right. He had insisted there were four to start with. So how...?

"I—I can't explain it." He shook his head. "This place is worse than the fun house at the carnival. But didn't you say last night there was one boarded after insisting there were none to start with?"

"Yeah, I did." Sally tilted her head and looked over at the windows. "But I'm certain none were boarded when Abby and I got here."

"Maybe this place is haunted or something," Cohen ventured.

"Ghosts haunting a church?" Sally snickered. "The Holy Ghost is here, but He's certainly not haunting the place."

"Rev, you explain it. You're the preacher here," Cohen insisted.

"As far as I'm concerned, the only boarded window is the one we boarded in the middle of the night. Wasn't it Abby who said we see with the eyes of our faith, and you see with your natural eyes?"

"You're right, I did," Abby said, her eyebrows raised at Cohen.

"So, if I see with my natural eyes, this church really is a burned out shell. Hannah, what about you? What do you see?" Cohen pleaded.

"Daaaa-ad, don't put that kind of pressure on me. I didn't see it exactly as you did when we got here, but neither did I see it like Sally and Abby did. I felt the warmth of the stove before you. But—it's odd. How can a boarded window break? I helped clean up the glass."

"Like I said before, I see with the eyes of my faith," Abby said. "I prayed for God to provide and He did. Cohen, maybe you're seeing this place from your brokenness."

Cohen jumped out of his seat. "Now see here. You don't know the first thing about my life, so don't go talking about me as if you do. I'm not broken!"

"I didn't mean to say you were. We all have wounds in our lives, things that have hurt us. Me included." Abby calmly turned to the stove to stir the food cooking in the cast iron skillet.

Cohen was too upset to sit back down. He turned to Hannah, who smiled weakly at him and sipped hot chocolate. Then he looked at the reverend whose face was unreadable. He turned back to Hannah. He stroked her hair back away from her face and squatted to meet her eyes. "Hon, how's your head? Feeling better?"

"A little. My shoulders are fine, but my head still hurts. The Tylenol's made it manageable."

"Okay. Keep me posted."

"If, when you hit the eight-hour point, you want more Tylenol, just let me know," Sally offered.

Hannah grinned. "Thanks, Sally. I will."

"That reminds me, Joshua," Sally said. "You cut your hand moving the pews yesterday. How's it today?"

"Completely healed." The reverend held out his hand for all to see. No scab, no mark of any kind.

"Let me see the other hand," Cohen insisted. Reverend Salem complied. "I can't believe it. It's like you never even cut your hand!"

"Cohen, it's not that you *can't* believe; it's that you *choose* not to. Believing always comes down to choice."

"I'm not sure I understand that," Hannah said. "Can you explain?"

"If the storm stopped this very minute, would it require belief for it to be real?"

Cohen pondered that for a few moments. Apparently so did everyone else because no one ventured an answer.

"It's not a trick question, folks. Seeing doesn't require believing. What you *can't* see always requires believing." The reverend took Hannah by her shoulders. "Have you ever seen Jesus?"

"No."

"Do you believe in Him?"

"Yes."

"And you believe in Him why? Because someone gave you unequivocal proof?"

Cohen watched as Hannah's eyes lit up and a grin spread across her face.

"I believe because I *choose* to believe. Thanks, Joshua!"

"God healed my hand. You can see the proof." The reverend dropped his hands from Hannah's shoulders and turned around to face Cohen.

He held both hands out, palms up. "The proof is right here, Cohen, so it isn't a matter of not being able to believe, you are choosing not to."

"All right, all right, you made your point," Cohen grouched. "God is your healer. And I need to wake up from this nightmare."

"Cohen," Rev said, "don't make the mistake the Israelites in the desert made. 'How long will these people reject Me? And how long will they not believe Me, with all the signs which I have performed among them?' After witnessing miracle after miracle they still refused to believe in God. Can anyone tell me what happened to them?"

Cohen threw an icy stare in Sally's direction. "I'm sure you know."

Sally zipped her lips and crossed her arms.

"Except for Caleb and Joshua, all those over twenty didn't get to enter into the Promised Land," Abby said. She took a step toward Cohen. "Don't refuse for the sake of refusing or because your pride is wounded. God has provided everything we need for life, and He has the answers you need for your business, but you can't access any of it if you don't first have faith and believe."

"What is this, gang-up-on-Cohen day? Just let me think!" He turned and walked to the south side of the church where the windows weren't boarded. He tried to stare out into the white landscape, but only saw his reflection staring back at him from the window.

The image startled him. He looked ninety-three, not fifty-three. Deep wrinkles creased his forehead, his eyes, his mouth. But it wasn't his physical appearance that upset him. The fear in his eyes screamed the fright of a terrified animal. Bankruptcy bore down on him like the storm raging outside. Reverend Salem made a strong argument about belief being a choice. He tuned his ear to the continuing conversation playing out behind him.

"Hannah, do you know what your name means?" Rev asked.

"No, I don't."

"It means 'God is my strength.'"

"Oh wow, I like that!"

"Abigail means 'my father is joy,'" Abby said.

"Joshua, do you know what my name means?" Sally asked.

Cohen perked his ears. He itched to know that one.

"Sally is a diminutive of Sarah. And Sarah means 'lady, princess, noblewoman.' I'm sure you know she was the wife of Abraham. Abigail was King David's wife. And Hannah was the mother of the prophet Samuel. Fine strong names for fine strong women."

A memory occurred to Cohen and he spun around. "Hannah. My mother suggested that name. She was a woman of faith. Do you remember her taking you to church when you were little?"

"Yes. Grandma's the reason I believe."

"Sorry about my temper." Cohen offered an apologetic smile to Abby. "If lunch is ready, let's eat. Can I help with anything?"

"No thanks. Sally and I have it. Take a seat."

He took his place at the table and let his memory wander while Hannah, Abby, and Sally gathered dishes, drinks, and the food.

An ugly anniversary was right around the corner: ten years since his wife left him after eighteen years of marriage. Maybe that's what had his emotions on a roller coaster ride. Nothing about life had been the same since.

Was Abby right? Was he a broken man?

Chapter Sixteen

"I will bless the LORD who guides me." Psalm 16:7a NLT

Once lunch was finished, we all seemed to be at odds on how to pass the time. No one wanted to play cards, and so we each found a small bit of private space to occupy. Cohen took up residence at his window, staring forlornly out at the continuing storm. Hannah lay down for nap. Abby retreated to the kitchen and Joshua to his office to pray.

I thought about playing solitaire or reading a book or my Bible. If it wasn't still so stormy outside, I might have chosen to go out and build a snowman. Hadn't done that in ages, and hadn't God just told me to enjoy the day? I chuckled to myself as I recalled Cohen's comment about me always being prepared. I wasn't as prepared as he thought. If I'd had a notebook, I could have started writing the book I'd been talking about for a decade but never managed to start.

I curled up on my pew, wrapped my blanket around me, and mulled over the existence of my biological family. Had my brother been adopted by a family in Scottsbluff? My real parents were dead, but did I have any aunts or uncles? If so, they'd probably all be well into their eighties by now. I went to the kitchen.

"Hey, Abby?" I said as I entered. She occupied the one chair we'd left sitting in the kitchen. "You mentioned our parents are dead, but do you know anything about our grandparents or if we have any aunts or uncles?"

She leaned back in her seat. "No, I don't. That thought never occurred to me. Karl's file is pretty thick. I wonder if he found that kind of info? Surely, if he had he would have told me. Maybe he can help us locate our biological family."

"If we can discover our original name, that will make the hunt a whole lot easier." I leaned back against the counter. "I'm so excited about the idea of a brother. Do you think he remembers us?"

"I doubt it. Mrs. Randall said he was three when your mom adopted you." Abby stood. "Let's go sit at the table. It'll be more comfortable."

"I thought all she said was that he was three years older than us," I said as we walked to the sanctuary and took a seat at the table. "I don't even know how old I was when I was adopted."

"You were under one. You were the first adopted, and Karl said I was still a baby when Mom and Pop adopted me."

"How do you know I was adopted first?"

"Think it through logically. Pop said in his video if he'd known about me, he would have adopted us both. I don't believe the orphanage would have hidden a sibling relationship between any of us, which means you and our brother had already been adopted when Pop adopted me. Otherwise, I'm sure he would have kept us together."

"Do you think our brother has tried looking for us?"

"Maybe."

"Here's another thought." I rubbed my eyes. "If our parents had siblings or their parents were still alive, why didn't one of them take us instead of us ending up in an orphanage? Does that mean our grandparents were dead or did no one want us?"

"Now, Sally, don't even go there. I know your father made you feel unwanted, but don't project that onto every possible relative we might have. Our grandparents might have been in ill health or too old to take on three young children."

"Yeah, you're probably right. But aren't you excited about finding our brother?"

"Sure I am. But you grew up an only child, so I'm sure your excitement runs deeper than mine." She side-hugged my shoulders. "Let's take one day at a time and trust God to lead us to our brother. God is already paving the way."

"That's true. He led us to Sarah and then to Mrs. Randall, didn't He? I'll let you go back to what you were doing."

Abby went back to the kitchen, and I turned my thoughts to my adoptive parents. I searched my memories for the good times. If I could reclaim the good, they'd replace the bad. There had to be some somewhere. Before Mom died. I could barely recall her face. I had no pictures of her to keep her fresh in my memory. Had my father ever taken any pictures? Maybe Mrs. Randall had some. I'd have to ask her.

That my father had a will and money left me nonplussed. He'd been in prison over a year before I got his letter telling me that fact. At the time, I was in Paris serving at the American Embassy.

One question after another bombarded me. Thinking about my parents stirred up all the negative memories—my father's abusive words and cruelty, and the trouble I'd gotten into when I lashed back at him. Mrs. Randall's words about Mom's anguish over having to choose between us taunted me as well. One tormenting thought after another raced through my mind. Like a merry-go-round circling round and round, going faster with each revolution. I jumped up off the pew, hoping to stop the spinning thoughts. My sudden movement startled Hannah awake.

"I'm sorry, Hannah. I didn't mean to wake you."

"That's okay. If I sleep all afternoon, I won't be able to sleep tonight." She stretched then left for the bathroom.

I reached for my phone to check the time, then remembered I had turned it off to conserve the battery. I never thought about how often I relied on my computer or my phone to tell me the time. I traipsed to the kitchen where a battery-operated clock hung on the wall. I glanced at the clock, then walked back to the sanctuary.

I needed to take control of my thoughts instead of allowing them to control me. I knew reading my Bible would help me do that. I grabbed it from under my pew and sat down to read until it was time to cook dinner, some two hours away.

I turned to Psalms. Lord, let Your Word bring peace to my spirit, soul, and body.

I thought bedtime would never come. The day had been unusually quiet. Little was spoken during dinner, and afterward the silence reigned on. My father's abusive words and my mother's anguish at having to choose between the three of us troubled me all afternoon and evening.

Now as I lay on my pew in the darkness of night, my heartache grew acute. The moment I closed my eyes, God's reminder from the night before rang in my ears. *My mommy loved me. I don't care if my father doesn't. I'll hate him like he hates me.*

Merely thinking the words caused my stomach to burn. I had unwittingly made a vow to hate my father. How had that impacted my life, and how had I carried so much hate all my life without realizing it?

Now both my parents were dead, and I'd never find the answers I needed. Then I remembered the letter Mr. Nathaniel had given me. I searched my purse as quietly as I could and located it. *Sally*, in large shaky letters, stared at me. My hands shook as I tore open the envelope and pulled out the letter. Several minutes passed before I plucked up the courage to unfold the paper and read it by the glow of the stove's fire.

Dear Sally,

I'm dying. When you get this letter, I'll be dead. I reckon I should have written this years ago and sent it while there was still time for us to reconcile. But I couldn't bear to have you visiting me in prison.

I can't blame you for distancing yourself from me. My behavior was atrocious. Your mother's death drove me to depths of evil I never knew existed in me. I couldn't seem to stop myself no matter how much I wanted to. But as the apostle Paul said 'I don't really understand myself, for I want to do what is right, but I don't do it. Instead, I do what I hate.'

My father was quoting the Bible?

Drove me even to murder. But what the Devil meant for evil, God used for good. I found Him while here in prison.

Hot tears welled in my eyes.

God has forgiven me. I hope you can. I'm so sorry for how I took my grief out on you. For all the horrible words I said and the abuse. I pray that one day we'll meet again in heaven, and that I'll be able to say these words to you personally. I'm proud of the woman you've become despite me.

Love, Father

I dropped the paper and it floated to the floor.

A wave of conflicting emotions overtook me, nearly suffocating me. No more trying to please him. No more trying to earn his love. No more trying to prove I was worth being called his daughter. He was a man who found himself caught in the responsibility of taking care of me. A responsibility he'd taken on to make my mom happy. Financially, he fulfilled his role, but he'd never been emotionally invested in me as his daughter. Our own stubbornness and pride had kept each of us from reaching out while there was still time to reconcile.

The realization of this struck me like lightning. I tried to focus on the crackle of the fire, the moan of the wind outside, its whistle as it penetrated the tiniest of cracks in the building—any sound as long as it would distract my thoughts.

I had stopped trying to prove myself to my father years ago. But now I realized I'd spent all my adult life proving myself to others, proving I was worth loving. What did it matter what others believed about me if I myself didn't believe I was worth loving? The time had come to free myself of this burden.

I stood and draped my blanket around my shoulders. I tiptoed to the front of the sanctuary, sat with my knees up, and wrapped my blanket snuggly around me, hugging my knees.

"God, I want to forgive. I thought I had. Why does it still hurt so much?" I whispered. I ached to pour out my burden at the foot of the cross in this peaceful little country church. The four people sleeping on the pews some twenty feet away kept me in check.

"Sally?"

The voice startled me and I jerked around, upset that someone was intruding on my privacy.

"Joshua, you startled me." I drew a deep breath through my nose and wiped my silent tears from my cheeks.

"I'm sorry. I didn't mean to."

"You look rather like an angel in the glow of that candle you're holding. But a gentle angel, not scary or intimidating like those in the Bible."

"Yes, Michael and Gabriel are fearsome warriors."

I marveled at his words. He spoke as though he'd actually seen those archangels.

"May I join you?" He directed his gaze to a spot beside me.

"I…yes. Maybe you can answer some questions I have."

"I'll try." He crossed his feet and eased himself into a cross-legged position, then set the candle on the floor in front of us. "You've been crying. …For your father?"

"No…yes." I shook my head. "There's a lot of history to my present frustrations."

"There usually is. I'm a good listener."

I smiled. Joshua's presence comforted me from the inside out. I tried to imagine what his sermons must be like. Somehow I expected that even a reprimand from him would be like salve on an open wound.

"Abby and I are adopted…by separate families. My adoptive mom died when I was ten. My adoptive father turned to alcohol and started verbally and sometimes physically abusing me. He'd never been particularly fatherly even before that."

"I'm sorry to hear that."

"Only yesterday—seems like days ago—Abby and I learned we have a brother and that my father forced my mom to choose just one of us even though she wanted to adopt all three of us."

"Oh my."

"I've spent years trying to forgive my father for how he treated me. For some reason, I thought that when he died, I'd feel free. But I don't." I looked at Joshua. He appeared gentle yet powerful. Something about his demeanor seemed to pull at my pain, as though he beckoned me to open my heart to him.

"What has you bound?"

"Bound? What do you mean?"

"You said you thought you'd feel free. If you don't feel free, something is keeping you bound, tied up."

I frowned. "I'm not sure. I never asked myself that question. I've forgiven him...a hundred times over. Last night the Lord pointed out that I was still holding onto my anger. But..."

"But?"

"The pain of those years never goes away. The physical wounds healed, of course, but the emotional pain...it just keeps getting worse. He was supposed to love and care for me." I clutched my knees harder and tipped my head back in an effort to hold back my tears.

"Yes, our earthly fathers are meant to be examples of our heavenly Father. Sally, look at me."

I closed my eyes for a moment, then did as he requested. The same warmth that spread through me yesterday when I shook his hand washed over me again. He cupped my face and with his thumb wiped a tear that trickled down my left cheek. He closed his eyes and tipped his head up ever so slightly, yet did not remove his hands from my face. I knew he was either seeking God's guidance for this moment in time or praying for me.

I forced my muscles to relax. God, if I can't hear Your words on my own, say them through Joshua. I felt his hands leave my face and I opened my eyes.

"It's not that you haven't forgiven him. You have. Like Father pointed out to you, what you haven't done is let go of the anger and the pain. Instead, you've shoved it deep inside of you in an effort to get rid of it."

"I tend to do that with any emotional pain I experience."

"Hanging onto pain blocks Father's love from flowing into your spirit, as well as out from your spirit to others. And pain never stays buried. When it surfaces, you rehearse all those bad memories again and remember all the hurt. That makes the hurt grow stronger and then you shove it all back down again in an effort to get rid of it."

"That's...that describes it perfectly. I didn't know what else to do with it so I stuffed it."

"Shoving it down inside is a way of telling yourself it doesn't exist. But you need to acknowledge that emotion in order to bring healing to it. Instead of keeping it inside, hand it over to Father. Think of it as an offering. Present it to Him like the Hebrews presented their offerings to the priest at the temple."

A sense of awe overcame me as I gazed into Joshua's eyes. I marveled at how he called God *Father*. Calling God Father was difficult for me. It put me in mind of my own father, and I didn't like that. "Joshua, you make me feel like I'm in the very presence of Jesus."

"That's because Jesus lives in me, the same way He lives in you." He grinned. "Father's love came into your heart the moment you accepted Jesus as your Savior. 'He who believes in Me...out of his heart will flow rivers of living water.' All that Abba has for you to enjoy can't flow into your life because all the pain you're hanging onto stops it like a dam does a river."

I considered his words. Could it really be that simple? Had my own actions kept me from experiencing God's promised abundant life I so desperately sought? I realized I often expect God to act like my father. From now on I'd call God Abba or Papa instead of Father. Perhaps that would help me begin to heal and see Him for the loving Father He was.

Joshua tweaked my chin, bringing me back to the moment. He smiled and rose. "Remember, noblewoman, you are dearly loved. You have suffered from a broken heart much too long, but Father began to heal that when He rained down His love on you."

Joshua's words instantly drew me back to a day in August while I was at the Reynolds' ranch. God had done exactly that—His love had washed over me that day as if I'd been standing in a gentle waterfall. Joshua had no way of knowing that except God had revealed it to him. I smiled up at him, at the same time realizing God had used Joshua's words to speak to me just as I had asked Him to do.

"I'll leave now so you can spend some time with Abba." He bent down to retrieve the candle.

Before he could grab it, I rose and pulled him into a hug. Peace, comfort, and love cocooned me as he embraced me, and I wished the moment would never end. "Thank you, Joshua," I whispered into his ear, then turned back to the cross, knelt down, and bowed my face to the floor.

It was time to acknowledge my pain and let it go, but I sensed this wouldn't be the last time. Too many years and too many hurts had created layer upon layer. How deep were those layers and how long would it take to be free of them all?

Chapter Seventeen

"In all your ways acknowledge Him." Proverbs 3:6a NKJV

Cohen's second night at the church mirrored his first, right down to his struggle to fall asleep and Sally getting up in the middle of the night.

He watched her as she sat at the front of the church. He saw her lips moving, but heard nothing. Her animated movements indicated she was speaking to someone, but he saw only her. What a strange woman she was. She insisted the church had a beautiful stained glass window behind the pulpit; that there were no burned pews, no boarded windows. Yet today, she had finally acquiesced to there being a boarded window.

Maybe *he* was going crazy. That stove had been cold the first two times he touched it, yet after Sally poured hot coffee into his mug, he burned his fingers touching the stove again.

Abby purported that God provided everything they needed.

God.

Maybe He provided for Sally and Abby, but not for him. Instead, God had taken everything away. Ten years ago Cohen had been on top of the world. He'd made record commissions in his job that year. He and his wife owned their dream home. He thought they were happy, until…he returned home from work to find his wife, Paige, gone. All her clothes, all her shoes, all her toiletries, even the shampoo and toothpaste they shared. Gone. What she had left behind was her only child and a short note: I'm leaving. Don't try to find me.

Hannah cried herself to sleep every night for a month. How could he expect her to understand when he didn't? He thought Paige was happy. She had never expressed any dissatisfaction with their marriage. She gave every indication that she, too, was as content and satisfied as he was.

Every day he scanned the face of every brunette he passed on the street, looking for Paige. Scottsbluff was a small town; surely he'd spot her. After a year, he gave up, hastened on by divorce papers that arrived in the mail. He signed them quickly and shoved them into an envelope as if even touching the papers burned his fingers. He had mailed them to a Scottsbluff attorney, but that didn't necessarily mean Paige still lived in town. A month later he received the final dissolution notice from the county court.

Their church attendance had been sporadic at best before the divorce, but that's when Cohen stopped going altogether. He'd thrown himself into his business, worked hard, and built it into a thriving consultant firm. Several years of great success followed, yet even before the pandemic hit, he noted a downturn. He'd been fighting to recover ever since.

In the limited space of his pew, Cohen turned his back to the others and tried to shove the memory out of his mind. In turning, he realized the truth of Abby's words. He *had* turned his back on God.

Cohen woke to the scents of fresh brewed coffee and frying bacon. The smell reminded him of the Boy Scout camping trips he'd been on as a boy. He smiled at the memory. He felt at peace this morning. Maybe the realization he had come to last night brought some resolution.

He looked over at Hannah's pew. She was still asleep, but a pained look creased her usually bright face. He shifted his attention to the stove and Abby cooking breakfast.

"Good morning, Abby. My mouth is watering just from the smell of that bacon. Thanks for cooking."

"You're certainly sounding chipper this morning."

"Am I? Where's Sally and Joshua?"

"*Joshua* is it? When did you stop calling him Rev?"

He shrugged, his eyebrows rising in rhythm with his shoulders.

"Well, Joshua is in his office, and Sally is in the kitchen getting the dishes for breakfast."

He rose and made his way to the bathroom. When he re-entered the room, Sally and Abby were laughing about something over at the stove and Joshua sat at the table, sipping coffee.

"Good morning, Cohen," Joshua said. "Can I pour you a cup of coffee?"

"I can manage. Thanks anyway." He took a cup from the table, grabbed a hot pad, and went to the stove. As he poured his coffee, it struck him that even with the noise of laughter and conversation Hannah hadn't awakened. "Hannah?"

She didn't stir.

"Hannah," he spoke louder.

"Is something wrong?" Abby asked.

"Hannah isn't waking up." Cohen walked to her pew and gently shook her. "Hannah, wake up."

A long groan rumbled in her chest. Her eyelids fluttered but failed to open.

He shook her again. This time a bit harder. "Hannah."

Her eyes blinked open. "Dad? What are you doing?"

"Trying to wake you up."

"Why? It's not like we can go anywhere. Besides, my head and neck hurt so bad I barely slept all night." She leaned her head to one side and yelped in pain.

"Abby, can you help?" Cohen asked.

Abby signaled for Sally to keep an eye on the bacon and walked over to Hannah. She knelt in front of her. "You said you hit your head when you crashed. How hard and what did you hit? The dash?"

"No, I hit the window, but not hard at all. It barely left a bump on my forehead. Remember? You looked at it."

"Yes. It did seem superficial. I suppose it could be muscle strain."

"I couldn't get comfortable all night."

"You don't have any support to your neck," Abby said.

"How can we help her?" Cohen asked.

"I'm not a doctor, and a doctor would know best. In our limited capacity, I'd say pain killer and icing her neck. Plenty of rest. Maybe after breakfast we can check Google and see what we can find out."

"Do you think you can sit up long enough to eat breakfast? Some food might help," Cohen said.

"No, I don't want any breakfast. My head is pounding so hard right now I feel nauseous."

"I'll find a trash can or bowl to keep handy for you." Cohen dashed to the kitchen. When he returned with a big bowl, Hannah was sitting up, and Abby sat next to her. He set the bowl on the floor.

"I need the bathroom," Hannah said.

"I'll help you." Abby stood and helped Hannah up from the pew. Hannah staggered to the restroom with Abby working to hold her steady.

"This can't be good," Cohen said the moment Hannah was out of earshot. He began to pace the room.

"Don't jump to conclusions," Joshua said. "God's watching over her."

"Please don't start with all that faith stuff."

"Without faith, you have no hope of things changing."

Cohen stared at Joshua. Last night's realization pricked him. He had turned his back on God. Was he now ready to renew his faith? He didn't have an answer for that, so he turned his attention to Sally instead. She had finished frying the bacon and now cracked several eggs into the pan.

"Mm-mm, nothing like a fried egg sunny-side up." Sally scooped hot bacon grease over the eggs.

"Not the healthiest though." Cohen stopped his pacing long enough to turn his lip up at the grease-coated eggs frying in the skillet.

"You let me know what you want for breakfast tomorrow, and I'll see if I can find it the kitchen," Joshua said.

"Oatmeal with apples and cinnamon would be nice."

"So noted." Joshua gave a nod.

"I don't know about anyone else, but I'm beginning to feel a bit grungy. A hot shower would be nice. Can you do anything about that?" Cohen asked.

"Sorry, no. As often as I've been stranded here, I have thought about putting a shower in." Joshua laughed. "I'll let the board know next time they meet."

Hannah returned from the bathroom minus Abby. Hannah's face had regained some color, and she was moving more steadily.

"You look better already. Do feel any better?" he asked.

"Yeah. I threw up. That helped relieve some of my headache." She eased herself onto the pew and wiggled around to get comfortable. "Abby's getting me some ice."

Sally grabbed her bottle of pain killer from her purse under her pew, picked out two Tylenol from among the ibuprofen, and dropped them into Hannah's hand. Joshua got a glass of water from the kitchen, and Hannah gulped down the pills.

Abby returned from the kitchen with a towel full of ice in her hand and arranged it across the back of Hannah's neck. "Maybe after I take the ice pack off, I can roll up a blanket enough to create some support for your neck, and you can lie and rest for most of the day."

"That sounds good," Hannah said. "For now, I'm going to sit here with this ice and try to sleep. I'll let you know if I need anything."

Cohen arranged the blanket across Hannah's lap and around her shoulders in a way to help hold the ice in place.

"Thanks, Dad." She smiled wanly.

"Hannah, could I pray for you?" Abby asked.

"I'd like that very much."

Abby raised one hand into the air and laid the other on Hannah's forehead. "Dear Father, You are Jehovah-Rapha, our healer. Your Word tells us that by the stripes Jesus bore, we were healed. I call her healed. Relieve her pain. Thank You, Father. In Jesus' name, amen."

"Thank you, Abby. I'm so glad you're here."

"So am I, sweetie." Abby smoothed some wayward strands of hair off Hannah's face and kissed the crown of her head.

Cohen noted Abby's natural motherly instinct and smiled to himself. He stepped closer, leaned down, and kissed Hannah's cheek. "I love you, pumpkin. Everything's going to be just fine."

Did his words sound as hopeless as he felt?

Cohen hovered over Hannah until he was certain she had fallen asleep.

This was all his fault.

He grabbed the coffee pot and poured himself another cup. "While I'm at it, can I pour a cup for anyone else?"

"I'll take one." Abby set hot platter of bacon and fried eggs on the table. She kept it all warm by leaving the platter on the stove. Smart lady. He smiled to himself and moved to Abby's cup on the table and poured.

"Let's eat." Sally placed a plate of toast next to the bacon and eggs.

"Toast? How'd you manage that with no electricity?" Cohen asked.

"I laid it in a hot skillet." Sally smirked at him.

They all took a seat at the table and Joshua prayed. "Heavenly Father, thank You for another day. For Your healing work on Cohen's wrist and in Hannah's body, for provision in this storm, for warmth, safety, and food. Bless the hands that have prepared this food, and bless this food. May it bring nourishment to our bodies. In Jesus' name, amen."

"Speaking of warmth," Cohen said, "I noticed the wood pile is getting low."

They all looked over at the wood stacked next to the stove.

"Getting low?" Sally said. "I guess it's relative. There's at least a dozen logs over there. I didn't—"

"A dozen! Are you blind as well as crazy?" Cohen insisted.

"Now look." Sally pointed her empty fork at him. "I've had enough of your insults. You're as bad as my father was! Just because I see things differently than you do doesn't make me crazy."

"Hey, you two." Abby held her arms out toward Sally and Cohen like a referee parting two angry boxers in the ring.

"What does it matter how we each see the church, Cohen?" Joshua said. "Why does your perception have to be the right one and Sally's wrong?"

"I never said anything about being right or wrong."

"But that's what you're insinuating when you call Sally crazy," Joshua said.

Cohen searched for an answer. He looked at Joshua, then Sally, then Abby. Each stared intently back at him.

"But..." was all he could force across his lips.

"It's all a matter of perspective," Joshua said. "Four people on four different corners of the same intersection see the same accident. Each will describe the accident differently because they have each viewed it from a different position."

"But we aren't standing on four different corners. We're all standing in one church that's either burned out or it isn't," Cohen insisted.

"Dad, what does it matter whether the church is burned or not?"

"Hannah. I thought you were asleep. I'm sorry if our conversation woke you," Cohen said.

"Let it go, Dad. What matters is that we stay warm and fed during this storm, not who's right or wrong about what the church looks like."

Cohen sat dumbfounded. He remembered last night and his realization of having turned his back on God. Maybe he wanted to see a burned-out church because he was angry at God.

"'Out of the mouth of babes and sucklings hast thou ordained strength,'" Joshua quoted. "There's wisdom in Hannah's words."

"Look, this storm should blow itself out today," Abby said, "and whether there are five logs or a dozen, God will provide what we need until we can leave here."

"That storm was only supposed to last thirty-six hours." Cohen scooped a couple of eggs onto his plate. "It's forty-eight and counting."

"Abby's right. God will provide," Joshua said. "Cohen, I know you're on edge about Hannah and your business, but getting angry at Sally isn't going to solve anything. There's at least a full cord of wood stacked at the back of the church. If it makes you feel better, we'll bring more of it in after breakfast."

"Fine," Cohen huffed. He glowered at Sally, then over at Joshua. "I'll get that done after I finish eating. I'm sure I can manage with one hand."

Joshua's calm demeanor as he stared back at Cohen aggravated him. He searched Joshua's eyes for a hint of anger but only found a compassion that rattled him. He broke off his look and turned his attention to breakfast.

"So, Abby, tell me about your ranch." Joshua took a sip of coffee.

"It's not *my* ranch, exactly. Sally, my brother, and I have equal shares in it. My brother runs it along with his sons."

"What animals do you raise?" Joshua asked.

"We have Angus cattle, but we also breed and raise American Quarter Horses. My great-grandfather started the ranch with Texas Longhorns he and several others drove up from Texas. The ranch has been handed down through the generations."

"I can't imagine what it must be like to have that kind of family history," Sally said.

"But aren't you adopted, Abby?" Cohen asked.

"Yes, but I only just learned that this year. Besides, it doesn't matter if I have no blood tie. I'm a part of the Reynolds family. Their history is my history." She turned her attention to Joshua. "I grew up helping with all the ranching chores, but after college I took over our magazine, *Cattle and Cowboy*."

"*You're* the power behind *Cattle and Cowboy*?" Cohen's mouth dropped open.

"The power?" Abby snickered. "I manage the magazine, that's all. But you're not a rancher, so how have you heard of it?"

"I've had several Nebraska Angus ranchers as clients. Seems they're never without a copy."

"That's nice. It's always encouraging to hear the work we do is making a positive difference."

The conversation waned while everyone ate. The clinks of silverware echoed in the room. Cohen kept his eye on Hannah. The pained look from earlier was gone, and she appeared to be comfortably sleeping, albeit sitting up.

"Tell me about your business, Cohen," Abby said.

"I'm a marketing consultant. I help businesses with their branding and marketing."

"Oh, yes, Hannah mentioned that. Any particular industry you specialize in?" Abby asked.

"No."

"I can't imagine you not having enough clients." Sally joined the conversation. "Every business needs great marketing."

"True. I guess instead of hiring a consultant, they're hiring for in-house."

"But not every business can afford to take on more employees," Sally said. "I'm looking at possibly starting my own business. Give me your business card before we leave here. I might give you a call."

"Okay, I will." Given his rude attitude toward Sally, her words surprised him.

Hannah groaned, catching everyone's attention.

"Didn't you say something yesterday about 911 being available?" Cohen asked.

"Yes. They know we're here and about your injury. They said if any emergency came up they'd do their best to get help to us, even if they had to walk here to do it."

Cohen sighed and took another look at Hannah. "That's good to know. If Hannah gets worse, maybe we can call them for guidance on what to do or have them send help."

Abby reached over, squeezed Cohen's forearm, and offered him a reassuring smile. He smiled back. "Thanks, Abby. Like Hannah said, I'm glad you're here. But I'm really worried about her. We slammed hard into that ditch, but she seemed fine. I mean, she said she hit her head, but it didn't hurt at the time. She barely even had a bump."

"The jolt could have strained her neck muscles," Joshua said. "Or maybe it's whiplash."

"Wouldn't that have shown up yesterday?" Cohen asked.

"She did have a headache yesterday." Joshua reminded Cohen. "Just not as bad as it is today."

"She'll be fine. God is watching over all of us," Abby said. "You can't deny that, can you, Cohen?"

"Of course he could!" Sally blurted.

Cohen glared at her.

"Sorry. It just sorta slipped out." She gave him a sheepish grin, then took a bite of bacon.

Cohen eased back in his seat, letting go of his anger. "You're right. I could deny it, but I won't. When I walked into this place two days ago, I saw a burned out building that threatened to collapse in a soft breeze. The stove that cooked our breakfast today was cold. I proved that by laying my hand on it twice without getting burned. You saw that." He nodded toward Sally.

"Yeah. It totally flabbergasted me."

"Yesterday, Hannah stood admiring a stained glass window. All I see is a blank wall with peeling wallpaper. I can't deny we're warm and well fed." He squirmed in his chair. "I've wondered if I'm going crazy or if I'm dead and in hell or if I'm just dreaming all this."

"Let me assure you, you aren't dead," Joshua said.

"Abby, I need to apologize to you. I need to apologize to all of you." Cohen looked at each face, trying to read the emotions painted there—a mixture of stunned shock and questioning. He swallowed hard. "My behavior has been all over the board. Angry one minute, calm the next. I'm usually not like that, really. As I lay awake last night, thinking, I realized the truth of Abby's words. I did turn my back on God. But…well…I think I want to start over."

Chapter Eighteen

"Troubles multiply for those who chase after other gods." Psalm 16:4a NLT

Q nearly spit out my mouthful of bacon at Cohen's declaration. *I'm ready to turn back to God* isn't what I expected during breakfast. I choked down my food and spent several minutes coughing. The disdain he had displayed for God seemed well-rooted.

"Yeah, I know, shocking news." Cohen's words dripped with sarcasm.

"Not at all. You're on the road back." Joshua gave him a congratulatory pat to his shoulder. "What caused this turnaround?"

Cohen sat silently for a few moments, the rest of us happily peering at him.

"Several things, I suppose. This strange place." He swept out his left hand, his right arm still in Abby's makeshift sling. His eyes flitted around the room and he sniggered. "Abby's words. But mostly…I spent last night thinking back on my life and realized the point in time when I turned away from God. Now that I think about it a bit more, I guess I've blamed God for most of the bad things that have happened in my life."

"Why *is* that?" I said. "Why are people always so quick to blame God for the bad, but never give Him credit for any of the good? I've been guilty of that myself."

"Because the devil has done such a good job of deceiving people into believing that because God is sovereign, He's responsible for everything that happens," Joshua said.

"But God is sovereign, isn't He? And all-powerful. He could have stopped my father from abusing me. He could have stopped Cohen's business from failing. Why didn't He?" I finished my toast and washed it down with some coffee.

Joshua pushed his now-empty plate aside. "Yes, God was capable of stopping those things. But He gave mankind a free will. He desires that all people come to a saving knowledge of Him. Let me ask you, does everybody believe in God?"

"No," we said in unison.

"And if people refuse to believe, does God force them to?"

Again a unanimous no.

"If Cohen had sought God's help with his business, God would have given him answers. Did you seek Him for help, Cohen?"

He shook his head, mumbled something through a mouthful of toast and egg, and then swallowed.

"If God had given you answers without you asking, would you have welcomed those answers and accepted them?"

"I probably would have told Him to butt out." Cohen grabbed another slice of toast.

Joshua chuckled, his eyebrows raised as if to say *exactly right.*

"But *I* did cry out for help." Tears threatened me. Memories of my father's abuse and now his death played havoc with my emotions.

"I have no doubt your father knew what he was doing was wrong," Joshua sipped his coffee and continued. "But he still made the choice to do it. God doesn't intervene in someone's free will."

"Even it means that free will harms someone else?"

"I'm afraid so."

"But, Sally," Abby reached over and squeezed my hand. "God did help you. He provided your friend Sarah and her family, a safe place where you were loved and watched over."

I thought that through for a moment or two. "You're right. Mom asked Mrs. Randall to look after me. That was God's provision. I failed to see that then. I probably would have gotten into way more trouble than I did if it weren't for the Randalls."

"When you boil it down," Joshua said, "neither God nor the devil can force you do to anything. *No one* can force you."

I scoffed. "My father forced me to do a lot of things."

"Now wait a minute." Abby released my hand and crossed her arms. "It was your choice to obey or disobey."

I looked over at Cohen, expecting to see a smirk, but his eyes were wide with awareness. Awareness of what? I wanted to deny what Joshua and Abby had said but was unable to.

"Right again. I guess when I'm faced with two bad options, I don't really consider that a choice. I'm being forced to do something I don't like or suffer the consequences of disobedience. Two bad choices, but choices nonetheless."

We all sat staring at each other, apparently processing the truth of Joshua's words.

After several minutes of silence, I came up with an idea. "It's Sunday. Why don't we have a church service?"

"It *is* Sunday, isn't it?" Abby said. "But the noise might disturb Hannah."

"Actually, I think it's a great idea." Hannah rubbed her temples.

"You're awake." Cohen rose from his chair and walked over to Hannah. "I thought you were sleeping."

"I dozed a little." She pulled the towel of ice off her neck and laid it on the pew. "I don't know if Joshua is prepared to preach, but I think some worship time would be nice. After all, isn't that what Paul and Silas did after they'd been beaten and thrown into prison. Maybe some worship would help me feel better."

"Worship sounds wonderful." Joshua rose from the table. "Let's clean up from breakfast first." He walked to the back of Hannah's pew, pulled out a brown well-worn hymnal that matched the 1940s vintage of the church's furniture. He handed it to Hannah. "Here. While we're clearing dishes, why don't you pick out a song or two you'd like to sing."

She smiled up at him. "Sure thing."

The rest of us went to the kitchen. With all of us working together, it didn't take long to get wash the dishes, and we all trooped back to the sanctuary.

"So, Hannah, what songs have you picked out?" Joshua asked.

She smiled up at him, her cheeks a bit red. "I'm a little embarrassed. This hymnal is so old I only recognize is 'Amazing Grace.'"

"That's an excellent place to start." Joshua grinned. "We'll stay here by the stove, and you can sit or stand. Your choice. Who would like to lead out?"

"I will," Abby offered. "I sing in the choir at my church."

We each grabbed a hymnal and found the page, then Abby sang out the first few words and we all joined in. Next came "The Old Rugged Cross." Hannah sang out contemporary songs like "Goodness of God" and "King of Kings." Her voice rang steady and strong despite her current state of illness. One song after another leapt spontaneously forth. If we knew the song, we joined in.

I don't how long or how many songs we'd sung when a sense of peace descended on me. Surely it filled the whole church. I had closed my eyes during "Amazing Grace" and hadn't opened them since. I ventured a peek through one eye. Abby's arms were raised. Joshua was on his knees. Cohen sat next to Hannah, holding her hand. Everyone wore a smile.

The room grew quiet for a moment, then a clear tenor voice erupted from Joshua with "It Is Well with My Soul." I knelt as I sang and tears sprang to my eyes. I made no attempt to stop them. They were grateful tears, joyful even. A greater sense of the depth of Jesus' sacrifice and love filled me. The love that drove Him to the cross…for me. How could I ever doubt He loved me, or that He would fulfill the promises of His Word? His unrelenting love compelled Him to do so.

After worship ended, Joshua retreated to his office. Cohen grabbed Hannah's bag of ice now lying on the floor.

"I'll put this back in the freezer for later," he said.

"I'll roll a blanket to support her neck, and help her lie down," Abby said.

I flitted off to Joshua's office, got a concordance, and then went to the table to do some Bible study.

"Why the concordance?" Abby asked as I set the book on the table.

"I want to do a search on the words *forgive* and *inherit*. They seem to continually come up during my Bible reading."

"I'm going to give Chase a call if I can get a signal. I was checking for Internet access and noticed a voice mail from him. He's probably worried. Then I thought Cohen and I might talk a bit. We'll try not to disturb you."

"No worries. It's not like I'm preparing a presentation or anything," I insisted. "Speaking of Chase, do you mind if I sit in on your call?"

"Not at all. Is there something you wanted to discuss with him?"

"No. I guess I just want to make doubly sure he's okay with me being in Great Falls through New Year's."

"He's fine with it." Abby took a seat at the table and powered on her phone. "I've only got one bar, but I'll give it a try." She punched in the number and hit speaker. The ring pleasantly surprised us, and we waited for Chase to answer.

The phone barely finished its first ring. "Abby, I'm so glad to hear from you! Are you all right?"

"I'm fine. I got your voice mail. We're still stranded at the church, but we're fine. We're staying warm and well-fed. This storm is lasting longer than I think anyone anticipated."

"You mean it's still snowing?" Chase said.

"Uh-huh." Abby stared out the window. "It's hard to tell how much snow there is because of drifting, and who knows how long it will take for the roads to be cleared."

"How's Sally?"

"Fine. Survival is second nature to her, remember? She's here. I've got you on speaker phone."

"Sorry, Sally. I tend to forget your Marine training."

"You're fine, Chase." I smiled at Abby.

"I think survival for Sally started long before she joined the Marines." Abby rushed on before I could comment. "Chase, has Karl been able to find out anything about our brother?"

"I asked him to call me as soon as he had anything, and he hasn't, so I assume not. It's not like he's had a week to investigate things."

"Yeah. We're just excited to find out. Let's pray he finds something. I'd love to talk more, but I need to conserve battery power," Abby said. "Keep your prayers going. Goodbye for now. I love you."

"Love you too, Sis. Take care."

Abby clicked off the call then powered off the phone. She sighed. "I didn't realize until now how much I miss home."

"Maybe your pilot can pick you up in Scottsbluff and take you home while I stay and finish things with my father's lawyer."

"Oh no. I'm sticking with you. For now, let me check on Hannah and Cohen." Abby rose from the table and made her way over to Hannah.

I divided my attention between my Bible study and watching Abby and Cohen. Each were equally captivating. Okay, I admit it, I paid more attention to Abby and Cohen.

"Hannah's going to be just fine, Cohen." Abby smiled at him.

He looked so miserable, his brow covered in wrinkles, a big frown on his lips. His eyes emanated pain. Having never been a mother, I couldn't fathom the depth of his hurt, but I imagined Abby knew. She had nieces she loved and would probably be hurting as much as Cohen if it was one of them in Hannah's position.

"So tell me, do you have other children?" Abby asked.

"No, just Hannah."

"You mentioned your wife divorced you. Did you have joint custody?"

"Actually, I had full custody. Hannah and I came home one day and found Paige, my wife, had walked out on us both." Cohen frowned. "She left a note. *I'm leaving. Don't try to find me.* Huh! Hannah cried for a month. She was only ten at the time."

Ten. Same age as me when my mother died. I expect we had similar scars from our losses.

"I'm so sorry. Is that—"

"When I turned my back on God? Yeah." Cohen sighed.

"But now you want to start over?"

"I thought so last night, but now…if anything happens to Hannah…"

"But God didn't make this hap—"

"*I* did," Cohen blurted. "I was in hurry to beat the storm and get to Rapid City. I was driving too fast for the conditions and didn't see the curve in the road. I'll never forgive myself." Cohen shook his head and closed his eyes. He leaned over and buried his face in his hands.

I noticed his shoulders jerking and realized he was sobbing. Abby must have too. She wrapped him in a side hug. They sat that way for several minutes, then Cohen sat up, squeezed her hand that embraced his shoulder and smiled his thanks.

"How's your wrist feeling?" Abby asked. "You're moving it around like normal."

Cohen's eyebrows shot up and he looked down at his wrist. He moved it carefully back and forth, then slowly around in a circle. "Wow, it feels great. Like nothing ever happened to it. Guess I don't need this sling anymore." He slipped his arm out of the sling, lifted it off from around his neck, then laid it next to him.

I watched as Abby took his arm and pushed his sleeve up a bit. "Even the bruising has dissipated. Praise the Lord for His healing!" She pulled his sleeve back down. "I wouldn't do any cartwheels just yet."

"Yes, doctor." An ear-to-ear smile spread across Cohen's face, and they both laughed. Why did Cohen respond so differently to Abby than to me? But then again, I seem to readily butt heads with most men. I certainly riled Chase. From day one, we had sparred like bulls in the pasture.

"Tell me about Hannah." Abby shifted on the pew as she spoke. "Is she in college? Oh, wait a minute, I remember something about her going to Switzerland, wasn't it?"

"Yes. Apparently, they have some of the best universities in the world. So she tells me. I'm sure she's done the research. She wants to go into business and technology management."

"Good for her. Maybe right now simply isn't the time God has planned for her to go, but if it's in His plan, she'll get there."

Abby and Cohen spent the rest of the morning in silence, Abby ministering to Hannah when needed. Hannah slept fitfully and groaned at times. Her face often reflected the pain inflicting her. Eventually, Cohen slipped off the pew and sat on the floor next to Hannah in order to hold her hand, and Abby went to the kitchen.

I turned my attention back to my study. I discovered *inheritance* showed up 239 times and *forgive* only 56. Not that that gave me an excuse not to forgive, but I had anticipated the word would occur much more often. Even more interesting was the fact that *forgive* was equally split between the Old and New Testaments.

A smile came unbidden to my lips. God, You are so amazing. The detail You have put into Your Word! Help me understand the truths contained there.

It would take a lot of time to examine each verse and look at the original language. With nearly two months ahead of me at the Reynolds' ranch, I'd have all the time I needed to study what I had stumbled onto today.

Meanwhile, I believed a relationship was developing between Abby and Cohen. I was excited for her; she'd never been married. But at the same time, Cohen didn't strike me as a good fit for her. His long-running animosity toward God didn't bode well. Be not unequally yoked and all that. However, he had said this morning he wanted to turn back to God. Maybe Abby was the person God chose to draw Cohen back to Himself.

That was an intriguing thought.

I suppose I needed to give Cohen the benefit of the doubt. I was seeing him in unusual and very stressful circumstances. But then again maybe this was his normal behavior when he was stressed. Not a good thing as far as I was concerned. Cohen's rudeness didn't seem to bother Abby like it did me. When he sat on the floor next to Hannah and grasped her hand, I glimpsed a side of him that surprised me. Clearly, he loved his daughter deeply and was very worried about her.

I don't know how much time had passed when hunger pulled me out of study mode. I closed the concordance and returned it to Joshua's office. He wasn't there as I had expected, and I wondered where he might be. I made my way to the kitchen. Abby was preparing lunch.

"Whatcha fixin'?"

"I found some cans of vegetable soup in the cupboard, but I thought I'd add some extra veggies. Canned veggie soup tends to be on the watery side rather than hardy."

"Should we have sandwiches too? There's plenty of lunch meat, isn't there?"

"I expect so. You'll have to look."

"Have you seen Joshua?" I dug through the refrigerator for the package of ham I'd seen yesterday. Abby continued chopping some carrots.

"No, not since our worship time ended. Why?"

"No reason. I just figured he was in his office and he's not. How's Cohen doing?"

Abby looked up from her task and frowned. "I'm not sure. He's upset and reasonably so. He blames himself for Hannah's condition."

"Yeah, I heard what he said about causing the accident. But I doubt she blames him. She seems like a sweet kid."

"Yes, she does. I am concerned about her health, though. I didn't tell Cohen; I didn't want him to worry any more than he is. If she worsens this afternoon, I think it might be smart to call 911."

We finished prepping lunch in silence. Abby added the carrots she had chopped and some frozen green beans to a small pot of water and cooked them before adding them to the rest of the canned soup. I made several ham sandwiches and took them to the table in the sanctuary.

Cohen was still on the floor next to Hannah and still holding her hand. Hannah appeared to be sleeping comfortably.

"Cohen?" Abby stood at the stove stirring the soup. "Are you interested in lunch?"

"Yeah, but I think I'll let Hannah sleep."

"Would you mind letting Joshua know lunch is almost ready?" Abby asked.

"Sure." He rose from the floor and left the room.

I finished setting bowls and spoons on the table.

"I can't find Joshua," Cohen announced when he returned to the room. "He's not in his office or the restroom."

"That's odd," Abby said. "Where else in the church could he be?"

"I always said there was something weird about him." Cohen grabbed a sandwich, snatched a bite, and then placed it on his plate.

Abby ladled soup into our bowls and returned the half-full pot to the stove. We all sat and Abby prayed. The moment she finished praying, Joshua entered the room. His cheeks and nose were a deep red. He sniffled.

"Joshua, you're not getting sick, are you? Your face is so flushed," I said.

"I'm fine. I've been up in the belfry. Bitterly cold out there." He stood as close to the stove as anyone dared without sitting on it. "You guys go ahead and eat. I'm going to warm up first."

"What were you doing up there?" Cohen asked.

"The belfry is about twenty-five feet high. I thought it would offer an excellent view to observe the extent of the storm."

"And did it?" Abby blew on her soup.

"Yes and no." Joshua rubbed his hands together then held them close to the stove.

"Enigmatic as always," Cohen mumbled through a bite of sandwich.

Joshua appeared to ignore Cohen's ubiquitous rudeness. "Yes, in that I could see severe drifting and your SUV half-buried in the ditch, Cohen, but the snow is still so heavy I couldn't see past the road." He made his way to the table and grabbed his bowl, returned to the stove, and filled it full of steaming soup. He took his place at the table and helped himself to a sandwich.

"My car is half-buried?" Cohen groaned. "How much longer before we get out here?"

"I don't know, my friend," Joshua said. "God will make a way. By the look of the sky, I think the storm will end before nightfall. Say, you're not wearing your sling!"

"Yeah, my wrist is better."

"What condition is the road in? Completely drifted over? Could you tell how many inches of snow we've had?" I rifled off my questions.

"Slow down. I can only answer one question at a time." Joshua took several spoonfuls of soup before he continued. "I can feel the warmth of that soup all the way down. It's delicious, by the way. Thank you to whoever prepared it."

"I did," Abby said. "It's just canned soup, but I added some extras."

"What was that term people used several years back when a similar storm hit the country?" Joshua paused his eating and looked up, probably trying to recall the word he was looking for.

"Snowmadgeddon?" Cohen said.

"That's it!" Joshua pointed his finger at Cohen. "Describes it perfectly. Now to answer your questions, Sally. It's difficult to even tell where the road is, and there is plenty of drifting. From twenty-five feet up, it wasn't possible to tell how many inches we've gotten."

Cohen dropped back in his chair. "It could take days to clear the roads. How far out of town did you say you are?"

"We're five miles north of Ardmore, but these days Ardmore is a ghost town, a place for tourists to visit. Edgemont is the closest town, and that's just under thirty miles from here. I'm not sure where the closest highway maintenance department is. I know the weather conditions look rather bleak where we are, but that doesn't mean it's terrible everywhere else."

"The closest town is thirty miles away?" Cohen said. "Who drives thirty miles to attend church?"

"Enough do. I serve the rural community now, but there was a day when my congregation was mostly Ardmore residents."

A moan from Hannah diverted everyone's attention. Cohen rushed over, arriving in time to hold the bowl while she vomited. Suddenly lunch didn't seem to appealing anymore.

"Pumpkin, I'm sorry you're feeling so terrible." Cohen held Hannah's hair out of the way while she vomited again. When she was done, she lay back.

"Can I have some water to rinse my mouth?" she asked.

"You can have mine." Abby grabbed her glass from the table and took it over. "I haven't drunk from this yet." She handed Hannah the glass. "I'll get a napkin so you can wipe your mouth and a cool rag to put on your forehead. That might help ease your pain."

Abby left for the kitchen, and Cohen helped Hannah sit up and take a drink, then he left for the restroom with the bowl. Abby and Cohen returned together, and I wondered if they had been discussing the situation in the kitchen, out of Hannah's earshot. It was clear to me Hannah was ill. Was it the flu or was it due to her head injury?

"Is it too soon for more pain killer?" Hannah asked no one in particular.

"I'm sure it's too soon for more Tylenol. Some ibuprofen would be okay, don't you think so, Abby?"

"Yes, probably."

I dug into my purse, got my bottle of meds and dumped a bunch into my hand, then picked out two tablets of ibuprofen. I scooped the rest of the tablets back into the bottle. "Here you go, Hannah."

She swallowed the pills, then settled herself back on the pew. Cohen wrapped the blanket up over her shoulders and patted her face with the cold rag Abby had brought from the kitchen. "Hang in there, sweetheart. You probably just have a bad case of the flu."

Cohen sat with her while the rest of us finished our lunch. When Hannah began softly snoring, he rose and returned to the table. Fear radiated from his eyes, wrinkles etched his forehead, and his jaw was clenched.

"We've got to call 911," he whispered.

"But, Cohen—" Abby protested.

"Let's discuss it in the kitchen where Hannah can't hear us." He didn't wait for our response but trekked off without us.

This didn't bode well.

When I entered the kitchen, Cohen was circling the room like a wagon master preparing his wagon train for an Indian attack.

"What took you so long?" he said.

"Calm down, Cohen," Abby implored. "Sally and I grabbed our phones. Joshua's gone to his office to check the land line."

Abby and I turned on our phones. I watched the screen, hoping enough battery power remained to make at least one more call. I released the breath I was holding as the screen lit up and worked its way through the start-up program.

"I've got power!"

"So do I," Abby said. "But it will probably be hours before any help could get here."

"Better three or four hours than two or three more days. Who knows how bad Hannah could be by then." Frustration and anger oozed from Cohen's every word. He stopped his pacing long enough to look out the window into the world of white. "I'd have to step outside to determine how much snow we've got, but it looks deep."

Abby went up behind him and placed her hands on his shoulders. He startled at her touch. He turned to face her. "Abby, please. We've got to do something."

I marveled at how he had so quickly connected to Abby.

"I don't want to put other lives at risk unnecessarily." Abby frowned.

"Oh, my daughter's well-being is unnecessary!"

"That's not what I said. I'm just not sure she needs immediate medical attention."

That didn't pair up with what Abby had told me earlier. Why was she telling Cohen otherwise? Was she saying that to keep him from panicking?

"But you're not a doctor."

"No, I'm not, but I've seen plenty of head injuries. My brother did his share of bull riding in his younger days, and my nephews have been bucked off a horse plenty of times."

"I'd still like to call 911," Cohen insisted.

"And we can, but we need to give them an accurate assessment of Hannah's condition. They'll need that in order to determine the need and urgency," Abby explained. "She hasn't lost consciousness, nor has she been confused or disoriented. Those are the three critical symptoms of a head injury that demand immediate attention."

Cohen just stared at Abby.

"It's probably best that I call 911 from my phone," I said while the opportunity presented itself. "They have a record of my number and my earlier call."

I heard the back door of the church bang closed and moments later Joshua appeared, his cheeks and nose red again.

"The storm is clearing!"

"Yesssss!" Cohen whooped. Ear-to-ear smiles shone on everyone's faces. "Does that mean it's stopped snowing, because it sure doesn't look that way from here?" Cohen once again gazed out the window.

"It's hard to tell if it's still snowing or if it's just blowing snow." Joshua wiped his nose. "But the clouds are breaking up off to the north and west. I caught a glimpse of blue sky."

"Thank You, Lord." Abby looked heavenward, her hands clasped together as though in prayer.

Cohen leaned over the sink, his head down. He took several deep breaths. I watched his shoulders slump. Maybe he was beginning to relax now that our circumstances were improving. The room grew silent, and everyone stood staring at his back. Seconds ticked by, and I wondered what thoughts banged their way around his head. Eventually he straightened up and turned around. He looked at each of us.

"What are you staring at me for?" he asked.

"Waiting for your response, I guess." Abby shrugged.

"I still think we should call 911. Do you think they could tell us how long it might be before the roads are clear? I should at least get Hannah to an urgent care facility or an ER somewhere. And how am I going to do that with my car in the ditch? I have no idea as to the extent of damage it sustained."

"I'm certain these young ladies will be more than glad to take you and Hannah to the closest facility." Joshua blew his nose and then pocketed his handkerchief.

"Of course," I said. "If none of us can get a signal, maybe the 911 operator can contact a towing service for you. Your car might still be drivable, and—"

"Our conversation is a moot point unless we actually call 911," Abby said. "Let me assess Hannah's condition, then we can make the call."

We filed out the kitchen door, walked to the sanctuary, and watched while Abby bent down and checked Hannah. She was sleeping, and though her face didn't hold the severe pained look it had held earlier, her brow was creased in wrinkles, and her jaw looked clenched—a family trait? Abby placed the back of her hand on Hannah's forehead.

"She's not feverish, but the lack of that doesn't mean she couldn't have the flu. I hate to wake her, but I can't assess her pain level without ask—"

"Don't!" Cohen said in a loud whisper. "I expect sleep is the best thing for her. Maybe I've been overreacting, but Hannah rarely gets a headache, and never one so bad that it made her vomit."

Abby stood. "It's okay, Cohen. I'm sure we all understand your concern. Let's give her a little more time. Next time she wakes up, we'll assess her condition, and then make the call if necessary."

"And if she's still asleep when dinner rolls around?" Cohen asked.

"We'll wake her and go from there. Keep positive thoughts." Abby offered him a smile, though I doubted it gave him much reassurance.

We all returned to the sanctuary, and Cohen immediately checked on Hannah again.

Chapter Nineteen

"Be strong and of good courage; do not be afraid,
nor be dismayed, for the Lord your God is with
you wherever you go." Joshua 1:9b NKJV

Cohen knelt next to Hannah as she lay sleeping. With his fears about her at least temporarily relieved, he decided to survey the condition of his car. He'd take Abby's advice and think positively. Maybe he'd be able to still drive the car—if he could get it out of the ditch. But he'd hit the ditch hard enough to blow the air bag. That in itself didn't mean the car couldn't be driven. No matter what, repairs were needed but would wait until he got Hannah checked out by a doctor.

"Joshua, would you mind helping me? I'd like to walk out to my car and determine how damaged it is."

"Certainly. Bundle up as well as you can. It's cold." Joshua's eyebrows reached toward his hairline.

"Somehow I get the feeling that's an understatement. We've had such a warm fall, I never expected snow. My coat isn't a winter coat, but it'll have to do. I'll layer on some shirts." Cohen walked to his suitcase and began digging through it. He pulled out several undershirts, a long-sleeve Oxford shirt, and a cable-knit sweater, then walked to the bathroom to layer up.

When he returned, Joshua stood at the front door, holding with two snow shovels. He held one out to Cohen. "We'll need to do some shoveling to gain access to the inside of your car."

"Terrific." Cohen grumbled, then shrugged. "It is what it is, I guess. Let's go."

"Wait a minute," Abby said. Both men stopped and looked at her.

"Shoveling snow is going to put too much strain on your wrist."

Cohen held his hand in front of him and moved it in various directions. "It feels fine. If God healed it, why would He only partially heal it?"

"He wouldn't," Joshua said.

"Okay then. Besides, I've got to figure out how bad the car is, and I can't make that determination without digging it out."

"Yes, but it won't help matters if you re-injure yourself," Abby said. "Go easy and take breaks. Let your left hand bare the weight of lifting."

Cohen gave Abby a gentle smile and a nod of his head. "I promise."

He turned back to the door and donned the scarf Joshua offered him. He gazed out the window. Unlike yesterday, his car was now visible. The snow had let up considerably and the once-heavy cloud cover appeared much lighter. Twilight was only about two hours away. He doubted they'd see sunshine before then, but they might see stars come bedtime.

Abby and Sally moved one pew enough for Cohen to open a door. He and Joshua quickly stepped outside, and the door slammed shut behind them. "Joshua, how many steps to ground level?"

"Only three."

"I can't see any of them. I guess we'd better start by scooping the porch."

They started from where they stood. The side edges of the front porch were clearly visible. Cohen scooped in one direction and Joshua in the other. Thankfully the porch was small, not that they had to clear the whole thing anyway. With that done, the edge of the stairs was easily found. But with each step down, there was more snow to scoop. It took them twenty minutes to clear a path only as wide as their two shovels.

As Cohen stood at the bottom of the steps, the snow around him reached his knees. He lifted his foot high and took a cautious step forward, sinking up to his knees. He took another difficult step. He had at least ten yards to cover before he'd get to the car.

"Aaarrrg! With this much snow to get through, it could take me thirty minutes or more just to reach the car," Cohen hollered over the wind. "Is the ground even or do I need to be concerned about gullies?"

"No gullies. It's gravel, but it's a nice flat area for car parking."

Cohen looked at his car. Joshua wasn't kidding when he said it was half buried. They'd have to do a lot of shoveling before he could open a door and slide in behind the steering wheel. He trudged forward.

Chapter Twenty

"You guard all that is mine." Psalm 16:5b NLT

There was no question in my mind. Abby and Cohen were attracted to each other. The compassion oozing from Abby's eyes and the care glimmering in Cohen's as he promised Abby to take it easy on his wrist told me a bond between them had begun to form. I didn't know whether to be glad or sad. Did long distance relationships ever work?

God had brought us all together for a reason, and I was certain it went beyond our own safety. I half-smiled. A God appointment for Abby and Cohen?

I turned my attention to the guys painstakingly making their way out to Cohen's SUV. "I'd venture a guess the snow is at least eighteen inches deep. It's past their knees." I shifted my gaze to Abby who busied herself caring for Hannah. Her pained look had lessened but was still apparent in the crinkles of her forehead.

When I looked back out the window, I noticed the guys had stopped. They'd barely gone five steps from the stairway but now stood discussing something. Then, instead of moving single file, they were shoveling a path. Cohen was shoveling toward the car, and Joshua was clearing the area they had initially walked through. They'd be worn out by the time they got done.

I felt rather useless standing around watching everyone else busy doing something.

"Hey, maybe I can go to the car and listen to the radio for an update on the storm." I looked out at my car. "I'll have to do some digging to get into it. Why do I get the feeling that God stranded us here on purpose?"

"As they say, God works in mysterious ways. But we know one thing for sure: God will use it for good."

"I have to admit, this is good fodder for a book." I laughed. "I'm going to go help the men. They look like they could use it, and it'll be dark before too long. I'm sure Cohen will rest easier tonight if he's been able to assess the condition of his car."

"You're right about that. I'll hold down the fort and make sure there's plenty of hot coffee for when you all come back in."

"Abby, you're such a blessing." I gave her big hug, then put on my coat and stuffed my pant legs inside my socks. I rummaged through my winter emergency tub and dug out my hiking boots and changed from my tennis shoes. Next I grabbed a T-shirt from my suitcase and wrapped it around my head and face as a makeshift scarf. You'd think I was prepping to climb Mt. Everest. I retrieved the broom from the kitchen, then pulled my gloves on. I pulled the pew back from the door just far enough to inch through, then held the door shut until I was certain Abby had secured it again.

When I stepped outside, the frigid cold engulfed me and stripped the air from my lungs. A landscape of white and blowing snow met my eyes. I took a moment to let my eyes adjust, then examined the swath in the snow the guys had already made. If I hadn't known better, I'd have thought we were in the middle of the Arctic Circle instead of western South Dakota.

My little car stood forlornly with snow halfway up the doors. Unlike Cohen's SUV, my car was easily reachable. However, I couldn't see the edges of the frontage road that led to the highway. How was I going to get to the highway through all this snow without ending up in a ditch myself? I closed my eyes and tried to remember if there were ditches alongside the frontage road. I couldn't recall.

I scanned the area from my car to the road. The surface of the snow lay completely flat with no depressions anywhere that might indicate a ditch. I saw no snow stakes that might have marked the road, but neither did I notice any on the highway. Maybe it was too soon for highway crews to have put them up, or maybe this stretch of highway didn't rate them.

I turned my attention back to Joshua and Cohen and plodded through the snow, doing my best to step where they had. I hollered at Joshua. Startled, he looked up from his work.

"I'm here to help," I yelled. My voice got Cohen's attention, and he, too, stopped shoveling. Each labored to breathe.

"We only have these two shovels," Joshua said. "I don't know how you could help."

"I can't just stand by and watch." I shrugged. "I can walk ahead to the car. I weigh less than you guys; maybe I won't sink as deep."

"That broom is useless." Cohen shook his head. The scarf covered his mouth, but I imagined a smirk plastered across his lips.

"I can use the broom to clear the snow off your car."

"This snow is too wet for that, but if you want to freeze your tush off out here, go to it," Cohen said.

I knew in the semi-arid climate of South Dakota that the snow was often like powder, easily swept clean from the sidewalks. I'd done the task plenty of times as a kid. However, he'd already been scooping the snow, so he probably was right. "If it was my car instead of yours, I'd want all the help I could get."

They stepped to the side of the path they had cleared and I made my way past them, Cohen mockingly waving me through like a gentleman.

Lord, like Peter walked on the water, let me walk on top of this snow.

With my first three steps, I sank more than knee deep. I could feel the icy snow sliding into my boots and I shivered. At least with my pants tucked into my socks, it wouldn't find its way up my pants or melt against my bare skin.

Lord, help me.

I took another step and didn't sink quite as far. Each successive step got easier. Five minutes later, I reached the car.

Thank you, Jesus!

The driver side of Cohen's SUV had taken the brunt of the snow, so I started on the passenger side. I inched my way down into the ditch.

Would the vehicle start after sitting for three days in the bitter cold with the front end buried in snow? I had jumper cables, but even if I could get my car to the shoulder of the road, they wouldn't reach. Surely a tow truck could jump it if need be.

Thankfully, the back half of the hood was clear. The drift across the front end blended with the snow in the ditch. I had a swath of snow a foot high to clean off the hood. I took the broom and swiped at the bottom of the drift but met with too much resistance. I tried sweeping across the top. No go. The snow did hold too much moisture for the broom to be of any use. I set it aside, and using my arms like windshield wipers, began pushing away the snow. With each swipe, cold snow made its way up the sleeves of my coat and into my gloves. I stopped every few minutes to shake it loose. The task was slow going and hard work. But certainly not as hard as Joshua and Cohen's task.

By the time twilight descended, the guys had reached the car. They shared a high five and gave a whoop of celebration. And deservedly so.

"Hey, nice work, Sally. Thanks." Cohen observed the work I had accomplished. His voice carried genuine thankfulness. This guy's emotions yoyoed too much for me to figure him out. One minute rude and angry, then the next perfectly polite. He slipped into the driver's seat from the passenger side and started the car.

"Yes!" He turned the engine off and climbed out. "That's a good sign. I might be able to drive home."

I had managed to clear the hood and a good portion of the nearly three-foot drift behind the car. My fingers and toes were numb and my back ached from bending over so much. "I hope the wind doesn't undo all our hard work overnight."

"Now who's sounding like a pessimist?" Cohen taunted.

As I opened my mouth to retort, Joshua intervened. "Don't you two get started. Hopefully the wind will dissipate with the storm."

"Amen to that! Abby said she'd have hot coffee for us when we were done. By now she probably has dinner ready too. Maybe Hannah will be well enough to join us."

"I'll say amen to *that*," Cohen said. "I'm really concerned about her. She hardly ever gets sick."

I looked up at the sky as we prepared to go in. The snow had stopped and the clouds had finally cleared. I spotted an early star sending its cheery light down to us. "I'd say this was a storm for the record books. I loved snow days as a kid. I still love 'em."

Cohen shook his head. "Like I said, you're crazy." He pulled his shovel out of the snow and headed toward the church, effectively cutting off any comeback I might have.

I looked at Joshua who stood there with an ear-to-ear grin.

"I'm quite willing to admit I'm a little strange." I held my hands out palms up. "I mean, I like the smell of a skunk. How many other people can say that? But I'm not crazy."

"God made you uniquely you, and He loves you just the way you are." Joshua began making his way toward the church. "You're his warrior daughter, and back in August you claimed an inheritance far more precious than material wealth. Now you just need to discover its depth and embrace it."

"Warrior daughter? How did you—" I held up my hand. "No, don't tell me; I already know. God told you."

He nodded and continued on his way as I dropped behind him. I marveled at the way Abby connected to God, but Joshua seemed to have a relationship that paralleled Jesus'. What were those verses from the Bible?

I only do what I see the Father do and say what the Father says.

My soul ached for a relationship with God that was that intimate.

As I contemplated that, I remembered a verse from my morning study. "Lord, you alone are my inheritance, my cup of blessing." I stopped short. I'd read those same verses yesterday and was on the verge of revelation when a gust of wind had startled away the thought. Joshua was right. What I had claimed in Montana was very precious. I had allowed myself to finally believe I was my heavenly Father's beloved daughter. And with that revelation I realized I had never fully trusted God.

Every man who had ever said the word *love* to me only trampled on my heart. You could have knocked me down with a puff of breath—I expected God to do the same.

We must have all looked like cherry Popsicles when we entered the church. Abby fussed over us like a mother hen.

"Get out of those wet clothes and into some dry ones. Then warm yourselves by the stove. We certainly don't need anyone catching pneumonia."

"Yes, Mother," I joked as I stripped off my gloves, coat, boots, and socks. My toes and fingers had gone numb within the first thirty minutes I was outside. I knew the burning pain of thawing out was ahead of me.

"There's plenty of fresh hot coffee. That'll help warm you on the inside. Dinner will be ready soon."

"Thanks, Abby," Cohen said. I noticed a glow of gratefulness in his eyes. He stepped over toward Hannah and looked down at her. "How's she been? Any change?"

"She's been sleeping comfortably as far as I can tell, and she hasn't vomited at all since lunch time."

"That's good, right?" Cohen asked.

"Yes, I'd say so. If it was a bout of the flu, I think she's on the mend."

Cohen let out a sigh of relief. He made his way over to his suitcase and began rummaging for dry clothes.

I plucked two pairs of fuzzy socks from my suitcase and slipped them on, then grabbed a pair of blue jeans, a thermal shirt, and a sweater and made my way to the restroom. Joshua followed me, but then headed toward his office.

Once in the restroom, I struggled to pull off my wet jeans and shirt. My legs and forearms alike were wet and red with the cold. I wondered if taking some ibuprofen would lessen the pain of my toes and fingers waking up. Oh well. I gathered my wet clothes and trekked back to the sanctuary. Someone had pulled a pew closer to the stove, and Abby was busy draping coats, gloves, and scarves across the back of it to dry. I added my pants, shirt, and socks to the group. My leather hiking boots were already sitting at the foot of the stove. How long would it take to get the insides dry? I could hear the sizzle of ice as it melted off my boots.

"I've got dinner prepared; it just needs to cook. I didn't want to start it not knowing how long you'd all be outside," Abby said.

I sidled my bum as close to the stove as I dared and attempted to warm up. "Remind me before we leave here to give Joshua some money for all the food we've eaten."

"That's a wonderful idea. We certainly have eaten high on the hog for a little country church." Abby disappeared into the kitchen and quickly returned with the cast iron skillet filled to the brim with meatballs.

My backside now sufficiently warmed, I turned to face the stove. "Any rice or potatoes to go with that?"

"I boiled a pot of rice while you were outside. It's still plenty warm, and when the meatballs are cooked, I'll drain the grease and add a can of cream of celery soup to them." She smiled. "Swedish meatballs."

When Joshua returned he looked cozy warm in a pair of jeans and a flannel shirt.

"Do you live here at the church?" I asked.

He laughed. "No, but I learned the hard way to keep a good supply of extras for just such occasions. They happen quite frequently." He joined me at the stove, holding his reddened hands out to the heat.

Cohen returned and hung his wet things next to mine over the pew. Like me, he warmed his backside first.

Except for the crackle of the fire and the sizzle of the meatballs, the room was silent. Everyone appeared content, and Hannah looked to be on the mend. The storm had ended after raging for nearly three days.

As my body warmed, so did my toes and fingers. I did my best not to grimace at the pain shooting through them as the feeling came back.

My arms ached from all the work, and I knew they'd hurt even more tomorrow. No doubt Cohen and Joshua would be hurting tomorrow as well if they weren't already.

"It's dark. Did I sleep the whole the afternoon?"

"Hannah!" Cohen jogged to her side and knelt. "Are you feeling any better?"

"Compared to this morning, yeah." She slowly sat up. Cohen embraced her. "Dad, take it easy."

He quickly released her. "I'm sorry. Did I hurt you? It's just that I've been so worried about you. How's your head?"

"Not pounding, more like a hangover."

Cohen pulled his head back and his eyes bugged out. "How would you know what a hangover feels like? You're only twenty!"

"Come on, Dad. You can't tell me you never got drunk before drinking age. Besides I only did it once, and swore then I'd never do it again."

I noticed Abby and Joshua closely watching Cohen. Were they wondering, like I was, if he was going to blow up at her?

"We'll talk about it later, when we get home. For now, do you feel well enough for some dinner?"

"That's debatable. I think so."

"I'll heat you some of the soup left over from lunch. These meatballs will be too heavy for you," Abby said. She zipped off to the kitchen.

"The storm's over. We should be out of here sometime tomorrow," Cohen said.

Though I fully believed the snow crews might work all night, I wasn't going to burst Cohen's bubble and tell him it was unlikely we'd get out of here tomorrow. More like the day after. Abby returned with a small pan of veggie soup and slid it next to the skillet on the stove, then gave the meatballs a stir.

"These are nearly done. Sally, could you get the pot of rice from the kitchen and put it on the table?"

"Sure thing." I headed to the kitchen. Initially my toes ached with each step, but by the time I returned to the sanctuary they had stopped.

Cohen was helping Hannah to the restroom as I exited the kitchen.

Fifteen minutes later the five of us were sitting at the table, enjoying dinner. I was ravenous—all that work clearing snow from Cohen's car. Then it occurred to me—I hadn't seen Joshua's car.

"Joshua, where's your car? It's obviously not out front, and I didn't see one out back when I helped you bring in the wood either."

"I don't have one."

"Then how'd you get here?" Cohen asked.

"Someone dropped me off."

"Your heavenly Father, I suppose," Cohen said sarcastically.

"As a matter of fact—"

"Don't bother. You're as strange as this church." Cohen finished the last bite of meatball and rice on his plate, then rose, and took his dishes to the kitchen.

"How's that soup sitting, Hannah?" Abby asked.

"Okay, I guess, but I'm ready to lie down again." She stood, tottered to her pew, and plopped down.

The rest of us finished our dinner. Cohen returned from the kitchen and gathered the remaining dirty dishes.

"Thank you, Cohen," Abby said.

"You're welcome. I'll help wash too."

They trooped to the kitchen. Cohen washed the dishes and Abby dried. They bantered and laughed as they worked. I stood at the kitchen entry and watched. Romantic tension filled the air like a scene out of *Casablanca*. Romance like that only happened in the movies. I prayed Abby wasn't about to get her heart broken.

I walked back to the main room. Hannah and Joshua each read a book, albeit by the light of the hurricane lamps. The cozy warmth of the sanctuary and a full stomach made me sleepy. Add two nights with only a few hours of sleep and I was more than ready to call it a night. I knew full well I'd quickly be asleep if I lay down, and I'd probably wake up at two in the morning and not be able to get back to sleep. Stuff it. I stripped off my sweater and one pair of fuzzy socks and curled up on my pew.

As I lay there, my heartache grew acute. My grit and determination had gotten me through my teen years. No doubt, the Marine Corps had honed those features. But the more I thought about it, the more I realized Abby was right about the depth of my hardness. I might not have spent years in prison like my father had, but I was in prison all the same. A prison of my own making and I'd thrown away the key.

I squeezed my eyes shut, which forced a tear to dribble down the bridge of my nose.

Would I ever be able to fully trust God in all things?

Chapter Twenty-One

"For you will not leave my soul among the dead." Psalm 16:10a NLT

I don't know how long I'd been asleep when voices permeated my mind.

"We've got to call 911. She's worse now than this morning." It was Cohen.

"Yes, I agree," Abby said. I heard her digging in her purse, then a male voice I didn't recognize.

"911. What is your emergency?"

That was odd. How was I hearing the 911 operator? Abby must have her phone on speaker, but why?

"It's my daughter." Cohen again. "She's got a severe headache and has been vomiting."

I struggled to wake up. I tried to get up but couldn't move. I tried to speak but nothing came out. Was I dreaming?

"When did the headache start?" the operator asked.

"Yesterday morning."

"Did anything happen leading up to when the headache started?"

"We crashed into a ditch two days ago. She bumped her forehead on the window, but she was fine. Barely a bump and she wasn't in any pain."

"How long after hitting her head did the headache and vomiting start?"

"She had a slight headache yesterday, but today it got worse and the vomiting started."

"Sir," Abby chimed in, "she's never lost consciousness or been confused or disoriented."

"Those are good signs. Who am I speaking to?"

"I'm sorry. I'm Abby Reynolds. I've got you on speaker."

"Do you have medical training, ma'am?"

"No, sir. But I was raised on a ranch and learned a lot of first aid."

"It would be still advisable to get her to the emergency room. Would you like us to dispatch an ambulance or will you transport her?"

Cohen scoffed. "My car is in the ditch, and we're stuck out in the middle of nowhere, snowed in. I have no idea where the nearest hospital is even if I could get there."

Cohen's voice had elevated in volume and finally penetrated my sleep enough to wake me. I opened my eyes and sat up.

"Where are you located, sir?" The man's calm demeanor seemed to keep Cohen from panicking. Or maybe it was Abby's hand on his shoulder that calmed him.

"We're at Christ Community Church on State Hwy 71, five miles north of Ardmore, South Dakota," Abby said.

A long silence followed and I thought they'd lost the call.

"Hey, are you still there?" Cohen demanded.

"Yes, sir. I'm sorry. We'll dispatch law enforcement, a wrecker, and life support services from Edgemont."

"And how long is that going take?" Cohen looked over at Hannah who was currently vomiting into a bowl. I walked over to her.

"Sir, I'm sorry that's impossible to say. Hwy 71 is the last highway to be cleared—"

"You mean to tell me we have to wait until a crew decides it's time to clear the highway?"

"No, sir. That's not what I mean at all. Snow crews have priority routes. Hwy 71 is rarely traveled and is the last to be cleared."

I saw Cohen's mouth open again, but Abby quickly placed her fingers over his lips, effectively stopping him from interrupting.

"It's doubtful any of that highway has been cleared yet. As I said, help will be dispatched immediately. They'll go as far as they can, and, if need be, switch to ATV to get to you. I'm sorry, sir, but it could be several hours before help arrives."

"How far away is this Edgemont you mentioned?" Abby asked.

"With good road conditions, about a thirty minute drive. Hot Springs is a little farther. Sir, what is the make, model, and color of your vehicle?"

Cohen looked at Abby. He had one eyebrow raised. "Why do you need to know that?"

"So I can let emergency service personnel know what to look for since we don't have an exact location on you."

"Oh, okay." His anger deflated. "It's a red Ford Escape."

"And look for a silver Chevy Cruze in the church parking lot," Abby added. "The church is white with a tall steeple and a bell, and it's on the east side of the highway."

"Thank you, ma'am. That's very helpful. Do you have any other questions?"

Abby looked at Cohen who shook his head. "No, we're good."

"Don't hesitate to call back if you need to," the operator said.

"Thank you." Abby ended the call and turned to Cohen. He huffed several breaths and ran his hands through his hair.

"Hours!… Hours!" He threw hands in the air. "Anything could happen in that time."

Hannah had stopped vomiting; I set the bowl on the floor and stood. "Let's take her to Jesus."

"What?" Cohen scrunched his forehead so hard his eyebrows nearly met. "Take her to Jesus? What are you talking about?"

Take her to Jesus? Did I really say that?

"Do you mean pray for her?" Abby asked.

I shook my head and thought. "No, I mean take her to Jesus…to Joshua. Joshua is really Jesus." I wasn't making sense even to myself. Was this all a dream?

"Joshua is Jesus? Sally, you're crazy!" Cohen yelled.

"Dad, stop!" Hannah grasped her head in her hands. "You're making things worse."

He hurried over and knelt in front her. "I'm sorry, honey. Let me help you lie back down."

I looked around the sanctuary for Joshua. "Where *is* Joshua?" I whispered to Abby.

"I don't know," she whispered back. "Sally, what do you mean Joshua is Jesus?"

"Abby, what can we do?" Cohen approached us, cutting off my opportunity to answer Abby's question. "It's going to take hours for help to get here."

"We're doing everything we can." Abby walked to Hannah who lay curled in a fetal position on the pew. "How's your head?"

"It's always better after I vomit. But it hurts so bad, I want to die." Tears trickled down her cheeks.

"We need to get some water into you. Cohen, get her a glass, and I'll go empty this." Abby picked up the bowl and headed to the restroom. I got some Tylenol for her.

Cohen ran off but quickly returned. Hannah sat up, took the glass, and took several slow sips, then swallowed the pills. When she was done, she set the glass on the floor and lay back down. Cohen arranged the blanket around her shoulders and smoothed her hair away from her face.

"An ambulance is on the way. Hang in there."

"My head feels like it's going to explode," Hannah sobbed.

Abby returned with the now-clean bowl and placed it within easy reach for Hannah.

"Is there anything more we can do to help her?" Cohen asked.

"We've done everything we can, except…" Abby said.

Cohen looked expectantly at Abby. I knew what she hesitated to say—to pray for her healing.

"We need to take her to Jesus," I reiterated. It seemed like those were the only words I could utter.

"What do you mean?" Cohen hissed through gritted teeth.

###

I buried my face in my hands to think a moment. Having had my share of migraines, I knew the agony Hannah suffered. I stared at her awash in the warm glow of the fire in the stove. After several minutes the room seemed to transform itself. Sunlight permeated the roof. The walls disappeared. Clamoring people invaded the quiet of the sanctuary. What was happening?

I did a 360, observing my surroundings. Trees and bushes I didn't recognize grew from a hard and otherwise barren ground. Palms trees dotted the hillside. I wandered among the crowd. Men and women of varying skin tones milled about me. They were clothed in dingy white robes with satchels slung across their shoulders. This must be a dream, but how? Cohen was part of the crowd.

"If you do not forgive, neither will your Father which is in heaven forgive you your trespasses."

I searched for the voice. Men, women, and children surged forward. As I worked my way through the throng, excitement rose within me. I speculated on where I was and *when* I was. When I cleared the crowd, and entered the house, the Bible scene before me of the paralytic lowered through the ceiling, confirmed my suspicions. I had to be dreaming, but it felt so real.

The heat of the sun warmed my face and penetrated my shirt. The stench of unwashed bodies assaulted my nose. I watched as the conversation continued.

"Which is easier, to say 'Your sins are forgiven you,' or to say, 'Rise up and walk'? But that you may know that the Son of Man has power on earth to forgive sins," Jesus turned to the paralytic, "I say to you, arise, take up your bed, and go to your house."

And the man rose, took his mat, and left, all the while praising and glorifying God. As he departed, the crowd disappeared.

I took a step toward Jesus. "Jesus, I repent of my hatred and bitterness. I repent. I repent for not trusting You in every way in my life. Forgive me."

I took a few more steps, and when I stood directly in front of Him, our eyes met. Love radiated from His eyes and pierced my spirit. Time seemed suspended as I gazed back. He placed his hand slightly below my throat.

"Let go," He said.

I closed my eyes and concentrated on letting go of my hate and bitterness, my distrust of people and of God. As I recalled memory after memory, the painful moments of my life drained out and disappeared. With the pain now gone, I discovered my true inheritance: a depth of relationship with God like I never imagined, as well as a new family that exemplified God's love.

When I opened my eyes, Jesus said, "You are my beloved daughter in whom I am well-pleased."

I hugged His neck and He hugged me back. I didn't want to let go. When I did, I spotted Cohen at the doorway, Hannah in his arms. I waved my arm for him to join me. He shook his head. I made my way to him.

"Cohen, it's Jesus! He can heal Hannah, but you've got to believe, to have faith."

He opened his mouth but nothing came out.

"My head...please, Dad, please make the pain go away. I can't bear it anymore," Hannah implored.

"Do you want her healed?" I asked him.

"Yes."

"Then it's time to make that choice; it's time to believe."

He walked forward. Abby came in the door behind him. We all stood before Jesus.

"Jesus, please heal my daughter."

"If you can believe, all things are possible to him who believes," Jesus said.

"Jesus, I believe; help my unbelief!"

Jesus cupped Hannah's face and smiled broadly at her. He placed one hand across her eyes. "Be healed, my child."

I felt power surge through me at His words. What must Hannah have felt? I knew in that moment she was healed. She reached her arms up and began praising the Lord.

"I'm healed! I'm healed! Thank you, Jesus!"

Cohen set her down and she began to dance.

I gazed at Jesus. A warmth saturated my body. I knew without doubt He loved me beyond measure. Was this what heaven would be like? I didn't want to look away. When I finally turned from Him to rejoice with Hannah, I found myself back in the fiery glow of the sanctuary, my blanket still wrapped securely around me. Joshua stood quietly by the stove, but everyone else was asleep.

I threw my feet to the floor and stood. The back of my shirt was wet with sweat. I tiptoed to Joshua.

"The most extraordinary thing just happened," I whispered. "It was so real; surely it wasn't a dream. I...I...could I have been caught up in the spirit like the apostle John was?"

"With God, all things are possible."

Chapter Twenty-Two

"Do not be afraid; only believe." Mark 5:26b NKJV

Cohen stared at Sally as they stood in the sanctuary, hovering over Hannah. His doubt about Sally Clark's sanity disappeared. *Take Hannah to Jesus? Joshua is Jesus?* Clearly her elevator had plummeted to the basement. He stomped over to the window and stared out into the darkness, willing the ambulance to come speeding down the highway, siren blaring.

After several minutes of staring at his reflection in the window, a glow of light from behind him captured his attention. He turned around to get a better look. He couldn't spot Sally or Abby anywhere, but there was a soft glow of light near the pulpit that seemed to emanate from inside itself.

Where in the world is that light coming from?

He'd never seen anything like it and was strangely drawn by it. He wandered every corner of the sanctuary, looking for the source. Finding none, he went and stood next to it. It radiated no heat. What he did feel was a sense of peace. He wanted to step into the light but hesitated. He reached out his hand but jerked it back. He stepped back, closed his eyes, and shook his head.

"This can't be happening," he whispered to himself. "I am *not* going crazy. I am *not* going crazy." When he opened his eyes, he found himself in the midst of a crowd of people, and the sun shone so intensely he immediately closed his eyes against its brightness.

He stood reasoning with himself. *I'm the one who's crazy, or I'm dead and this is hell. But I thought hell was fire and brimstone.* As the noise of the crowd penetrated his thoughts and the heat of the sun warmed his back, he decided he must be dreaming. He slowly opened his eyes.

Trees and bushes he didn't recognize grew from a hard and otherwise barren ground. Palms trees dotted the hillside. He wandered through the crowd around him. Men and women of varying skin tones milled about him. They were clothed in dingy white robes with satchels slung across their shoulders.

"If you do not forgive, neither will your Father which is in heaven forgive you your trespasses."

He searched the area for the voice. Men, women, and children surged forward. He worked his way through the throng. When he cleared the crowd and entered the house, he spotted Sally. *That crazy woman is here? I'm in a dream from hell. But it seems so real.* The heat of the sun had warmed his face and caused him to sweat. The stench of unwashed bodies assaulted his nose.

He watched as a paralyzed man got up, took what he'd been lying on, and left the house, praising God.

Cohen spun around, away from Sally. Where was Hannah? Sweat dotted his forehead and trickled down the middle of his back. He scanned the crowd and found her and Abby. Hannah's face was very pale and she was crying. He tried to yell to her, but no matter how hard he tried, he couldn't make a sound.

That man could heal Hannah. He worked his way over to her, picked her up, and went back into the house.

Chapter Twenty-Three

"I will not be shaken, for he is right beside me." Psalm 16:8b NLT

As morning dawned, I felt disoriented and struggled to remember what day it was. I stared at the ceiling for several seconds before concluding it was Monday, our fourth day of being stranded.

Then memories of last night flooded in, sending tingles throughout my body. Goose bumps rose on my arms and legs. It must have been a dream. I closed my eyes and attempted to put myself back in Capernaum in that house with Jesus. I thought about the hate, the bitterness, and all the emotional pain I had let go. I thought about my father and his cruel words. The memories were still there, but the heartache that had been their constant companion all these years had disappeared. I sighed and whispered, "Thank You, Jesus," as I breathed out.

Whether my time there had been a dream or somehow real, the result was the same. Facing the memories and my emotions had washed away the brokenness of my heart. Jesus had healed those wounds.

Then I remembered Hannah had also been healed. I scanned her face as she lay asleep on her pew. A glow of contentment replaced the pained expression that had been so prevalent the last two days. Hallelujah!

I tossed my blanket off, stood and stretched, went to the bathroom, then headed to the kitchen to make coffee and some breakfast.

Before long, Abby joined me.

"Good morning. Up before everyone else as usual, I see." A big smile brightened Abby's face.

"I'm a morning person; no doubt about that. How'd you sleep?"

She shrugged—one of my habits. Had she picked it up from me? "Okay, I guess. I had the oddest dream."

"You too? Mine was more amazing than anything else." I busied myself laying slices of bacon in the skillet. She grasped my shoulders and gently turned me toward her, tilted her head and looked at me.

"Your face is glowing."

"Really?"

"Definitely."

"Abby, I had the most extraordinary experience last night. It had to have been a dream, but it felt so real, right down to the warmth of the sun on my skin. And the whole dream was in color! I rarely dream in color." I turned back to my work, all the while reliving that moment and hearing Jesus' words, *You are my beloved daughter in whom I am well-pleased.*

"Don't just stand there. Tell me about it."

"I let go of all my bitterness and hurt. I was healed, and by Jesus! And Hannah got healed too. Dream or not, I'll never forget—"

"Stop!" Abby grabbed my arm to interrupt my work. "I was there too."

Chapter Twenty-Four

"Create in me a clean heart, O God, And renew a steadfast spirit within me." Psalm 51:10 NKJV

When Cohen woke, the room was almost unbearably bright, and he knew the storm was over. A sigh of relief escaped as he rose from the pew and stretched. *Wow, this place looks...totally different in the sunshine.*

His mouth dropped open as he noticed, for the first time, the stained-glass window Hannah had admired. A rainbow of light flooded the room. He couldn't understand it. When he and Hannah had arrived, the place looked like it would collapse at any moment. And now...

Only one boarded window, the one the tree branch had crashed through. A large pile of wood by the stove. Pristine white walls as though freshly painted. Not a speck of charred wood to any of the pews or walls. No peeling wallpaper or exposed lathe and plaster.

And that beautiful stained-glass window.

Then he remembered last night's dream. Had the call to 911 been real or part of his dream? Being at a strange house, the crowd of people dressed in robes, Abby and Sally, and Hannah. No, that part had to be a dream.

"I had the oddest dream," he heard someone say from the direction of the kitchen. He'd describe his dream as weird. He debated whether to eavesdrop and decided he would. He walked to the hallway and stopped short of the kitchen doorway.

"It had to have been a dream, but it was so real, right down to the warmth of the sun on my skin. And the whole dream was in color! I rarely dream in color."

He recognized the voice as Sally's.

"Don't just stand there. Tell me about it." That was Abby.

"I let go of all my bitterness and hurt. I was healed, and by Jesus! And Hannah got healed. Dream or not, I'll never forget—"

"Stop!" Abby paused, and he ventured a look into the kitchen. "I was there too."

He stepped into view. "So was I."

Chapter Twenty-Five

"You will show me the way of life, granting me the joy of your presence and the pleasures of living with you forever." Psalm 16:11 NLT

We all stood staring at each other.

"Oh my," Abby said.

"That's an understatement." Cohen huffed.

"Were we all caught up in the Spirit?" I asked.

"Caught up in the Spirit? What's that?" Cohen looked at me, his forehead creased in wrinkles.

"It's a phrase found in the book of Revelation." Abby walked to the sink. "I've never heard it explained before, but I guess you could think of it like an out-of-body experience."

"When I woke up last night, my shirt was drenched with sweat," I said. "Joshua was standing at the stove, and I asked him if I could have been caught up like the apostle John."

"What was his answer?" Abby pulled five coffee cups from the dish drain and laid them on a tray.

"'With God all things are possible.'" I laid the piece of bacon I was holding into the skillet and turned back to Abby.

"I can see a change in your body, Sally," Abby said.

"I feel as light as a helium balloon."

"We need to write down every detail of what we can remember of our individual experience. And date it. The devil will try to fool us that it never happened." Abby picked up the tray and turned to head to the sanctuary.

"That *what* never happened?" Joshua asked as he entered the kitchen.

"We all seem to have had the same dream last night," Cohen said.

"It was no dream, Cohen. I was there too." Joshua smiled.

"But you're the one person I didn't see," I said.

"You'll remember if you think about it." He gazed at me, and the compassion in his brown eyes pierced my soul. The love in Jesus' eyes during my experience last night hit me like an ocean wave crashing onto the shore. It hit with such force I stepped back to catch my balance, nearly overwhelmed by the power of it. The emotion of both moments melded into one.

I hoped no one had noticed my reaction, but it appeared Joshua had. His faced took on a glow, and he grinned at me. I couldn't look away. Did no one else notice the glow illuminating his face?

"I don't recall seeing you anywhere," Cohen said.

"Me either," Abby echoed.

But I knew. Joshua and Jesus were one and the same. I'd keep that amazing revelation to myself for now. Cohen would scoff and call me crazy. I'd tell Abby after we left the church.

"It's impossible for us all to have had the same dream." Cohen started pacing.

"And I told you it wasn't a dream," Joshua said. "The Lord gathered us all into the heavenly realm."

"No way. That's ridiculous," Cohen insisted.

"But Hannah was healed," Joshua said. "Surely you don't want to insist that didn't happen."

Cohen's eyes grew wide, his eyebrows rose, and a smile slowly curled his lips. Had he forgotten about Hannah's healing? He turned to leave the kitchen, but Joshua seized his arm.

"You have to believe; have faith and act on that faith. Don't go into that sanctuary with any doubt in your heart."

Cohen stood staring at Joshua. Panic appeared in his eyes. "Joshua, help my unbelief."

Joshua smiled, put his arm around Cohen's shoulders and led him into the sanctuary. Abby and I followed. Cohen stared down at Hannah's sleeping form as we approached.

He turned to us. "Is it me or is her face glowing?"

A loud thud at the front doors startled us and woke Hannah.

"What's going on?" Hannah said.

There was more thumping on the door. Someone was trying to get in.

"This is the Edgemont Fire Department. Is there anyone in there?" a man yelled. He followed it with more banging.

"Yeah, we're here!" Cohen hollered back. "Hang on, we need to clear the doorway." Cohen and Joshua rushed to one pew and moved it out of the way while Abby and I moved the other one. A gust of cold air blew in as five firemen entered, their faces red with the cold. Once everyone was in, Joshua and Cohen replaced one pew to keep the doors shut.

"Are you the folks who called 911 last night?" a fireman asked.

"Yes, I did," Cohen said. "I thought maybe I dreamt it."

"No, sir. We've had quite a time getting through the snow. You reported a possible head injury. Who's hurt?"

"It's my daughter."

"But I'm fine now." Hannah sat up. "Dad, I had the strangest dream…Jesus healed me!"

Cohen knelt in front of her. "It wasn't a dream, honey. We were all there."

"Excuse me, sir." A paramedic stepped next to Cohen and indicated for him to move aside. "We need to ensure your daughter is okay. Fill us in on the symptoms." The two paramedics began their routine.

"Is there somewhere we can talk while they work?" another fireman asked.

"Certainly." Joshua held his arm out. "Let's go to the kitchen."

"You gentlemen look as though you could use a good hot cup of coffee." Abby grabbed the pot, and we walked to the kitchen. Cohen stayed with Hannah.

Abby quickly filled the five cups she had pulled from the dish drain earlier, lifted the tray from the counter, and offered it to the firemen.

"Thank you, ma'am," the three men said in turn as each eagerly grabbed a cup.

"I'll take these out to the paramedics." Abby left the kitchen with the other two cups.

"It was quite a trek getting here. I'm Chief Schmidt, Edgemont Fire Department. Law Enforcement and a wrecker were dispatched as well, but they can't get through yet."

"Reverend Joshua Salem." He shook the chief's hand. "I pastor here. This is Sally Clark. The lady who offered you coffee is Abby Reynolds, Sally's sister. The gentleman in the sanctuary is Cohen Reed and his daughter, Hannah."

"How long have you folks been stranded here?"

"Since Friday," I said. "But we've been warm and well fed."

Abby returned, empty tray in hand.

"Yes, with you ladies cooking, we've feasted." Joshua rubbed his stomach. "What are the conditions like outside?"

"Freak storm, that was. Dumped a good two feet of snow on this little corner of South Dakota. Elsewhere not nearly as much. The snowplow should get through here yet today, and behind it the wrecker for that red SUV in the ditch.

"Can't imagine you have much of a flock, Reverend. You're out in the middle of nowhere."

"I manage, Chief." Joshua smiled. "Sally, Abby, why don't you cook up a big breakfast. We'll feed these men a hardy meal before they leave."

"That's not necessary, Reverend," the chief said.

"Of course it is," Joshua insisted. "You've come a long way in that bitter cold."

"I'll go check on the paramedics," the chief said. Everyone but Abby and I headed for the sanctuary. I turned back to the skillet of bacon I had begun preparing earlier.

"Wow! Do you think Chase will believe us when we tell him everything that's happened?" I laughed. "I'm still amazed myself."

"I don't think he'll doubt our words."

"I know God created us as relational beings, but I've kept myself very guarded in that arena. It's time for change. I wasn't comfortable about a romance with Chase. After last night, I'm okay with the idea."

"Now *that* he might find hard to believe!"

We had a hardy laugh then started breakfast.

The next hour and a half passed in a flurry of activity. Abby and I cooked breakfast. The firemen cleared the snow from around my car and Cohen's. The paramedics determined Hannah was fine, but recommended she see her primary care doctor as soon as she got home. When breakfast was done, there was nothing left except for us to wait for the snowplow to clear the road and the wrecker to arrive. The men from the Edgemont Fire Department prepared to leave.

"Thank you all so much for your help." I shook the chief's hand.

"Our pleasure, ma'am," Chief Schmidt said. "Thank you for breakfast. It'll keep us warm on our return trip."

Joshua and Cohen moved the pew to let them out. Already the sun had begun to warm the air. We shut the door, replaced the pew, and watched the firemen trek to their utility vehicles and drive off.

"Time to clean up." I rubbed my hands together. "Let's get these dishes washed, Abby."

"I'll help," Hannah said.

"No, you just rest," Cohen insisted.

"I'm fine. Didn't you notice how many pancakes and eggs I ate?"

He laughed. "Enough to make up for the last two days. Go ahead."

We all set to work, no doubt, each of us excited at the thought of finally being out from under the grip of the storm.

"Hey, listen. I think I hear a truck." I rushed to the door and looked out. "It's a snowplow," I hollered to the others. We watched from the front door windows as the plow scooped the snow, flinging it high into the air and to the side of the road. Shortly after, the police and wrecker arrived. Cohen donned his coat and went out to his car to meet them.

He returned with the policeman, while the man from the wrecker began to assess Cohen's SUV.

"Are you people okay? I don't have any food, but I've got some water I can share, and you can warm yourselves in my car," the policeman said.

"We're fine. Reverend Salem kept us well-fed and warm. Why do you ask?" I answered.

"Reverend Salem? Reverend Joshua Salem?" he asked with surprise.

"Yes. Why?" Cohen frowned.

Joshua had dismissed himself to his office immediately after breakfast as he had done each morning we'd been here.

"This place is a wreck. Can't imagine how you've stayed warm and fed. The church burned about thirty years ago. I remember it well because my parents and I attended here. There was a big event to celebrate fifty years for the church." The policeman looked around. "Used to be such a pretty little church, with a stained-glass window behind the pulpit."

We all looked at each other, Cohen's face the most incredulous of all, his eyes wide as saucers and eyebrows reaching to his hairline.

"Burned? I was right all along. I told you two this place was a wreck."

"But, Dad…" Hannah gazed around the sanctuary. "Look at it. It's beautiful."

"Beautiful?" The policeman looked around at the sanctuary again.

"It's a long story, Officer," Abby said.

The policeman sniffed the air. "Is that coffee I smell?"

"Sure is. Sit down and have a cup while you tell us the story of this church." I offered him a seat at the table.

He glanced at his watch. "I could use some caffeine. Been up since 3:00 a.m. But first I need to get the details of that accident."

"Do you need cream or sugar?" I asked.

"Black is fine. Thank you."

I went to the kitchen for a cup, returned to the sanctuary, and poured him some coffee. "I think maybe we need to hear about this church before you take your report."

He looked at each of us, then nodded. I guess the varied expressions of surprise and confusion on our faces convinced him. He took a deep breath and readied himself for his story.

"Reverend Salem founded and built this church in May of 1942, not long after the attack on Pearl Harbor. I guess the war prompted more people to church. Anyway, in '92 he'd been preaching here for fifty years and was still going strong even though he was in his eighties. Attendance had dwindled to about twenty or so, mostly families that had helped the reverend get the church going. All the same, the elders decided to hold a celebration. I ate so much pie I nearly made myself sick." He shook his head as he remembered, a grin creasing his lips. He slurped down some coffee, then continued.

"Don't remember how the fire started, but as I half recall, it might have been arson. Being a young teen at the time, I don't know all the details outside of the fact that those in charge decided not to repair the damage. Reverend Salem died about thirty days after the fire."

"Wow." Hannah's mouth gaped open. "Then who's that man who's been calling himself Reverend Salem?"

"I'll dash down to his office and grab him," I said.

"Cohen, go with her," Abby insisted.

A frustrated look crossed his face, but he didn't argue. We made our way to the reverend's basement office.

"I told you this place had been burned," Cohen said as we made our way down the stairs.

"So you did, but aren't you glad Abby and I insisted otherwise?"

He merely grunted his response.

"Joshua," I called as we approached the office. But we found it empty. "Maybe he's in the bathroom."

We looked down the hallway toward the restroom. The door stood open.

"Reverend Salem?" Cohen called. We both stood with bated breath, waiting for him to come out from somewhere in the basement. When he didn't emerge, we returned upstairs.

"We can't find him anywhere," I said as we entered the sanctuary.

The news from the policeman and now Joshua's absence shocked us all. We sat staring at the policeman for several minutes. He cleared his throat. "You folks okay?"

"Yeah, it's just that…well…" Cohen faltered.

How could any of us tell the policeman what had transpired here since Friday?

"I'd better finish this accident report. Can you give me your details, Mr. Reed?" He and Cohen completed the information and the policeman left. The tow truck driver pulled Cohen's car from the ditch and determined it was safe enough to drive despite the blown air bag.

Somehow, I couldn't leave the little church without putting it back in the same condition I'd found it. We returned the table and chairs to the kitchen and put all the pews back in the proper place except for the ones at the front door. Abby doused the fire with a pitcher of water.

We all repacked our suitcases and moved them to the trunks of our cars. This experience had given us a common bond. I felt as though we were family even though we barely knew each other.

"Let's stay in touch," Hannah said. "Would that be okay with you, Abby and Sally? And you can let us know if you find your brother."

"Of course." Abby briefly hugged Hannah.

"Yes, I'd like that too." Cohen pulled out his wallet and handed both Abby and me a business card. He pulled a third card out and flipped it over. "Abby what's your phone number and email?" He jotted the information as Abby gave it. He looked at me.

"I'm sure you don't want the crazy woman's phone number."

"I—"

"I was only kidding." I rattled off the number.

Everyone hugged each other, then Cohen and Hannah made their way out to his SUV. Abby and I waved from the doorway as they drove south to Scottsbluff and the comfort of their home.

I turned to Abby. "We still have time to make the appointment with the real estate agent. Isn't God amazing?"

"He's more than amazing. Let's say a prayer before we leave."

"Good idea." We clasped our hands together and Abby prayed.

"Thank You, Jesus, for Your provision during this storm. Let us, Cohen and Hannah included, never forget the miracle that occurred here at Christ Community Church, or the most amazing miracle of all, Your death on the cross that redeemed us. Amen."

"Amen. When we're done with business in Scottsbluff and we get to Great Falls, I'm going to do some research and see if I can find any pictures of Reverend Salem online."

"Why?"

"Even though I'm convinced the reverend really was Jesus, I want to see a picture of him. We experienced a miracle!" I threw my hands in the air.

"Yes, we did. I can't help but wonder how this will impact each of us. I hope Cohen is able to fully embrace God again."

We stood in the doorway and turned to take one last look at the sanctuary that had kept us so warm and safe in the middle of the blizzard. "What do you see, Abby?"

"I see a beautiful little church, just as it was when we first entered it." She looked at me. "How about you?"

I walked down the steps and looked up at the steeple. "I see a tall steeple with a bell, and inside a pot-bellied stove, pristine white walls, pews with red cushions, and a beautiful stained-glass window."

And that's how I would always remember it.

Dont' stop now!

Follow Sally on her journey to *Embracing Her Inheritance*, book 3 of this series.

A Miracle, a Brother, and a Love She Never Expected...Will Sally Embrace Her True Inheritance?

Sally never imagined her life would change so drastically at fifty-eight. A brother she never knew? A miracle in a blizzard that's making the news? Sally is overwhelmed, and the skeptical media is stirring up doubt.

Determined to track down her brother, Sally's journey hits another roadblock—the blossoming feelings she has for Chase Reynolds, Abby's adoptive brother. Chase has been nothing but supportive, but Sally fights her emotions, burdened by a past marred by her adoptive father's cruel words. As she struggles to believe she's worthy of love and happiness, Sally must face her deepest fears.

Embracing Her Inheritance is a heartwarming story of faith, healing, and second chances. Will she find the courage to embrace both the family she's been given and the love she never expected? Or will her past hold her back from the life—and inheritance—she desires?

Buy *Embracing Her Inheritance* today and encounter the answers.

Discover More

If you enjoyed this book, get Debra's short story *Mystery on Maple Hill* for free by subscribing to DebraLButterfield.com. You'll also get updates on coming releases and her Wednesday Word, an email with Bible teaching and encouragement.

Acknowledgments

Thank you to the St. Joseph, MO 911 services and to Maria King of the South Dakota 911 Coordinators Department for their assistance in how 911 calls are handled.

To Marilyn Scholz and Erin Taylor Young who gave me so much insight and feedback. To my beta readers, Troy Jackson, Kathy Bunse, Pat Butterfield, Orene Taylor, Sue Hodges, and Angie Clayton, and my critique group who helped me fine tune this story.

And to my editor, Connie Williams, whose advice helped me polish this story to its best.

About Debra

Debra L. Butterfield dreamed of being a writer since she was a pre-teen. As a pre-teen she wrote Star Trek fan fiction. Fulfillment of her writing dream began when she was forty-five years old and Focus on the Family hired her as a junior copywriter. In 2005, she moved to Missouri and in 2006, she stepped into the world of freelance writer.

She is the author of ten books, which include *Claiming Her Inheritance, Discovering Her Inheritance, Self-editing & Publishing Tips for the Indie Author, Unshakable Faith,* and *Carried by Grace.* She has contributed stories to numerous anthologies. Her magazine credits include CBN.com, *Susie, Live, The Vision,* and *On Course* online, writer's newsletters, and guest blogs.

Debra is a second-generation US Marine and lifetime member of the Marine Corps League.

She enjoys the outdoors and, oddly enough, likes the smell of skunks. (Her kids always tell her to take a deep breath whenever they smell one.) Now living in Missouri, Debra has three adult children and two grandchildren.

Discover more at DebraLButterfield.com.

Claiming Her Inheritance

She just inherited a fortune... but the
strings attached could unravel everything.

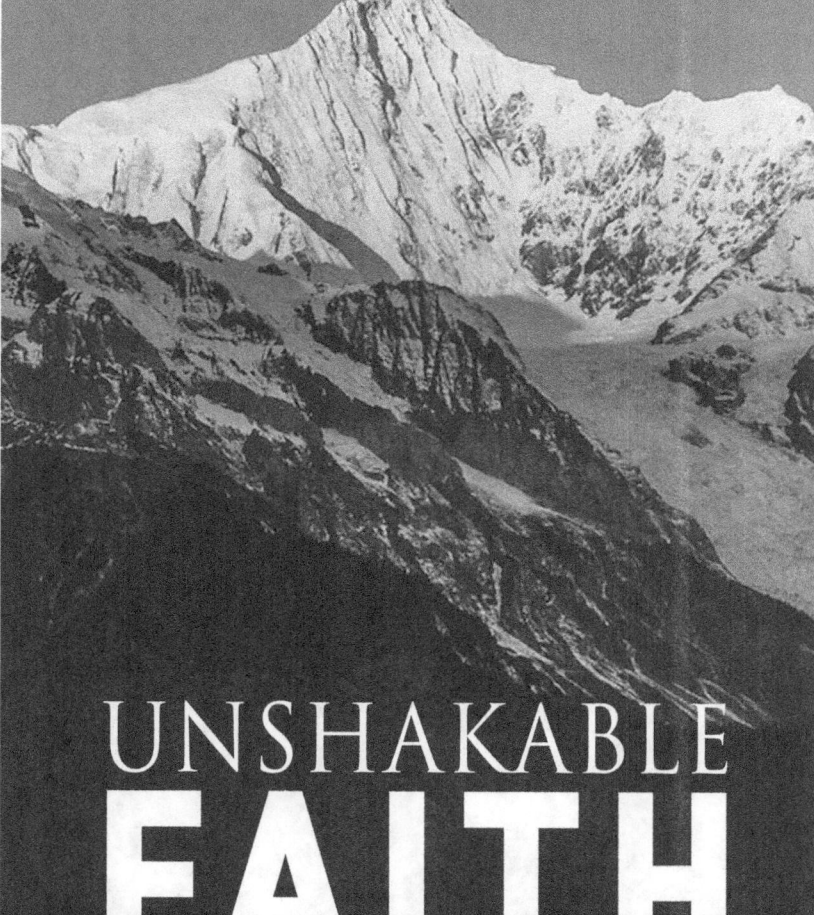

UNSHAKABLE
FAITH

Living Strong in the Kingdom of God